THE
PHANTOM
FIVE

Other books by Connie Remlinger Trounstine

The Worst Christmas Ever
Fingerprints on the Table

THE PHANTOM FIVE

CONNIE REMLINGER TROUNSTINE

ARCHWAY
PUBLISHING

Archway Publishing books may be ordered through booksellers or by contacting:

Archway Publishing
1663 Liberty Drive
Bloomington, IN 47403
www.archwaypublishing.com
1 (888) 242-5904

Because of the dynamic nature of the Internet, any web addresses or links contained in this book may have changed since publication and may no longer be valid. The views expressed in this work are solely those of the author and do not necessarily reflect the views of the publisher, and the publisher hereby disclaims any responsibility for them.

Cover Illustration by Darrin Wilmes

ISBN: 978-1-4808-1761-6 (sc)
ISBN: 978-1-4808-1762-3 (e)

Library of Congress Control Number: 2015905777

Print information available on the last page.

Archway Publishing rev. date: 4/22/2015

To my editor, Joanne Mattern, who has always been there for me and believed in *The Phantom Five.*

CONTENTS

CHAPTER 1

THERE HE IS, MANNY KEEFER, scrappy point guard for the freshman University School Blue Jays team, playing in the most important game of the season. The scoreboard flashes University School 42, Brownville Central 44. Manny inbounds the ball to his best friend and guard, Felix Cann. Wally Baldwin, his second-best friend and team center, is making his way down the court. Felix dribbles the ball, instinctively looking to see if Wally is open under the basket. He is not.

Felix moves to his right, stops, and lets the ball fly. The ball hits the front of the rim, and Wally taps it in. University School 44, Brownville 44. The Brownville coach jumps up, calls time.

Coach Ellis is waiting as Manny and his teammates walk to their bench. "Okay, Blue Jays," Coach Ellis says, "hang tough. Play strong defense. Be ready for a rebound, in case they miss their shot." And then, eyeing each player, he adds, "Whatever you do, don't foul."

Manny, Wally, Felix, and the rest of the team and coaches lock hands and shout in unison, "Go!"

The Brownville captain throws the ball inbounds to their star player, who dribbles the ball, heading straight for Manny. Manny is the only object between his opponent and the basket. As the player pushes forward, Manny plants his feet. They collide. Manny falls to the hardwood floor.

The referee blows his whistle. He motions to the scorekeeper. "Foul. Charging."

Both teams walk to the opposite end of the court. Manny takes his position at the free-throw line. He can feel his heart beating as he looks at the clock. Only two seconds remain. If he makes the first and then second free-throw, his team wins. Unless the opposition makes a final Hail Mary basket so the game goes into overtime.

Wally and Felix give words of encouragement. "You can do it."

"Take your time."

Manny thinks of all the hours he practiced at the basketball hoop his father put up for him on the garage for just this situation: winning the game for University School. He takes a deep breath. Shoots.

Swish.

The ball goes through the net without touching the rim. He bounces the ball several times, takes another deep breath, and then lets the ball fly. This time, it rolls around the rim and then falls through the net. University School 46, Brownville 44.

Quickly, the Brownville guard throws the ball inbounds. Their star player bounces the ball, takes a couple of dribbles, and then heaves the ball hard as he can. The ball arches but falls well short of the goal. The buzzer sounds. University School wins.

The band plays; the crowd cheers. Wally and Felix rush up to Manny. Much to his surprise, they lift him up and carry him off the court.

"Manny, will you be home Wednesday evening? Manny, did you hear me? Did you hear one thing I've said?" His father's sharp, loud voice jarred Manny back to reality, back to his family's kitchen table.

"Ahh, mmm," he muttered, looking first to his father and then his mother, his sister Nora, and finally Aunt Etta, who bailed him out by repeating his father's question.

"Your father wants to know if you will be here Wednesday evening for the neighborhood meeting."

"Wednesday, gosh, I don't know. Basketball season starts this week. The coach could call a practice."

Everyone at the table was surprised to hear him mention basketball practice. His mother asked the question. "Manny, did the coach change his mind? You weren't the last one cut? Are you back on the team?"

"Sort of," Manny said. "Didn't I tell you? I volunteered to be team manager."

The look on his father's face told Manny he wasn't the least bit impressed that his son was the team manager. "I'm sure the team won't miss you for one night," his father said. "This is important. I've volunteered to be the air-raid warden for the district, and I want everyone in the neighborhood to know what they must do, particularly my son."

"Does President Roosevelt really think the Japanese would bomb America?" his mother asked.

"These are difficult times," his father said.

"And scary times too," Aunt Etta added. "You just don't know who the enemy is. A sign on the wall at work says, 'Loose lips sink ships.' I shake every time I see it."

"What does that mean?" Nora asked.

Before anyone could answer, his father stood up, looking at his watch. "We have five minutes to get to the trolley stop."

Manny was surprised and hurt that his father dismissed him so easily. But then, these were not ordinary times. In fact, nothing was the same for anybody anywhere since that day a year ago.

Manny remembered exactly what everyone in his family was doing on December 7, 1941, when the news of the Japanese sneak attack on Pearl Harbor was announced on the radio.

He had been sitting on the living room rug and reading his favorite newspaper comic strip. His dog, Duncan, who looked just like President Roosevelt's Scottish terrier, Fala, was snuggled up close to him, chewing on a bone Manny had slipped him under the dining room table.

"I'm next for the sports section," he had reminded his brother, Howard, who was sitting in the overstuffed chair, his face hidden behind the paper.

Nora was standing as stiff as a mannequin on a small stool in the center of the room while his mother quickly pinned the hem of her new dress.

His father, Aunt Loretta—who everybody called Aunt Etta—and Uncle Hubert were sitting at the card table in front of the fireplace, playing pinochle.

The radio in the corner of the room was tuned in to the Metropolitan Opera. Everyone was only half-listening until the excited, high-pitched voice of a newscaster had cut through the soothing music like a serrated knife. The next day, President Franklin D. Roosevelt announced that the United States was at war.

Manny didn't know then exactly what being at war meant. As the days and months wore on, he learned.

Nothing was the same.

Howard was one of the first in line to enlist in the Marine Corps. Manny tried to write to Howard every week, but he couldn't begin to tell him about all the changes or how he felt scared inside all the time.

Aunt Etta moved into Howard's bedroom after Uncle Hubert was drafted. She went to work at Ulson's Dry Goods Store, where she sat at a sewing machine forty hours a week, making uniforms for the soldiers.

Mom volunteered as a nurse's aide at Good Samaritan Hospital. The aides filled in for the registered nurses who were sent overseas. "Heaven forbid that Howard is injured, but if he is, I hope some good nurse will care for him over there," she said again and again to reassure herself and the family that Howard would be safe.

Now the only time the family was sure to be together during the week was in the early morning, before they left for work and school.

Manny promised he would be at the Wednesday meeting as his father, mother, and aunt hurried out of the kitchen on the way to the trolley stop. Manny's father hadn't taken the car out of the garage more than a half-dozen times since they all had taken Howard to the train station last year. Gasoline was rationed, just like flour, sugar, meat, and cigarettes.

When the cuckoo clock on the wall outside the pantry struck half past seven, the house was as quiet as a church, except for the sound of Nora's spoon hitting against her cereal bowl.

Manny sat down at the table across from her, encouraging her to eat a little faster because he wanted to get to school early and shoot baskets with Felix and Wally before class.

Manny's life with his friends had changed more drastically than his life at home. But he couldn't blame the war for those changes.

CHAPTER 2

F ELIX, WALLY, AND MANNY HAD been a trio for a long time. They all lived on Elm Hill Drive, with Felix and Manny next door to each other. Wally lived on the other side of the street in the next block.

The boys did everything together—swimming in the summer, playing football in the fall, and shooting hoops in the winter. They were a formidable trio on the basketball court. They played on intramural teams in the lower grades and were three of the starting five for the seventh- and eighth-grade and freshman teams.

But that all ended when Manny didn't make the sophomore team. He was the last person cut from the squad.

When Coach Ellis told Manny he didn't make the team, Manny felt as though he had been sucker-punched and tackled from behind at the same time. But he didn't let anyone know that. Before Coach Ellis could say another word, Manny asked if he could be the team manager.

Being manager was nothing compared to playing on the team, but Manny kept his feelings to himself. The worst day in his life, since Howard left home, was the day he'd been cut from the team. The second-worst day was the day he wrote to his brother and told him he didn't make the team.

He had promised Howard he would tell him everything that was going on. Not making the team was a major thing in Manny's life.

Howard knew basketball. He had been a star on his team at University School. Manny wanted to be just like his brother.

Howard responded to Manny's letter immediately.

"It's not your fault that you didn't get the genes to make you six feet, one inch tall like I am," Howard wrote. "Besides, I think you're the best free-throw shooter I've ever seen. Remember when you won the most important game of the year with your perfect free-throw shots? You have the touch. As a manager, you can help the guys out when they're in a slump. It takes nerves of steel at the free-throw line. And under pressure, you are cool, little brother. Help the other guys."

Manny hadn't thought of it that way. But it was true. He did take after Mom's side of the family. He was named after her father, his grandfather, Emanuel. Luckily for him, he was nicknamed Manny. He had dark hair and brown eyes like his mother had. He was skinny. He couldn't gain a pound no matter how much he ate, and he ate a lot. But he could hustle. He thought that should count for something. But Coach Ellis didn't see it that way.

He was well coordinated even though he wasn't tall. Hours and hours of practice helped make him a deadeye shooter from the free-throw line. That was why he, Wally, and Felix had made such a great team. Manny was quick and scrappy. As a point guard, he knew how to plant his feet just when the heavier, taller players were driving to the basket. Instead of the two-point basket, the referee would whistle the charge foul.

Manny's percentage at the free-throw line was an awesome 95 percent. But now his height and size were against him.

Manny kept Howard's letter, along with all the other letters he received from him, in a shoebox under his bed.

Manny tapped his fingers on the table, hoping the noise would remind Nora he was waiting, not so patiently. She paid no attention to him.

He picked up the morning newspaper and turned to the sports section.

A bold headline leaped out at him. "New Editor 'The Brew' Promotes High School Sports."

Manny hadn't heard about a new editor. He started to read aloud. "In this time of great national stress, basketball will be a great mental relaxation for players and fans alike." He paused.

"Mmmm. What do you think of that, Nora?"

She didn't seem to hear. He looked down at Duncan, who was lying next to his chair. The black-haired dog with a funny beard looked up at him with soulful eyes.

"Good, boy. You're listening." Manny leaned over and took a piece of crust that Nora had left on her plate. "Sit, Duncan," he said. The dog obeyed. Manny dropped the crust into the dog's mouth.

Manny continued reading. "Plenty of mothers, dads, and other enthusiasts will jam the rafters of gyms throughout the area again this year in an effort to get their minds off the war, a war that is worrying everyone."

"I don't like the war," Nora whispered. "Howard and Uncle Hubert are thousands of miles away. Mommy's gone all the time. Now Daddy's going on a raid. I'm afraid."

She started to cry.

"Don't cry," Manny gently scolded. "Dad's not going on a raid. He's an air-raid warden. That means … I'm not sure what it means, but we'll hear all about it. We must be brave, too, like this sports editor says." He held up the paper."

Manny quickly read the last paragraph of the news article. "This new editor promises to print the box score of every game played in the tristate area. All you have to do is call in the results of your game and I'll print them."

8

Manny tore the article out of the paper and put it in his geometry book. He had to tell Felix and Wally about this.

And wait until he wrote to Howard. He'd be able to send lots of clippings from the daily newspaper about his alma mater's basketball team. If he called in enough stories about University School, maybe he would get a byline. He could see it now: "University School the Best Small School Team in the City," by Manny C. Keefer.

CHAPTER 3

THE SCOREBOARD CLOCK HIGH ABOVE the bleachers in the corner of the gym beamed five seconds as Felix dribbled the ball across the centerline. He looked to his right but passed to Wally, who was waiting on his left.

Wally, his lean body gleaming with sweat, showed the ball to his opponent's face. Then, as quickly as an arrow released from a bow, he dribbled past the gangling guard. He stopped short of the basket, pumped the ball, waited for the guard to jump up then come down.

Swish.

The buzzer sounded. University School 57, Madison Academy 56.

Manny jumped off the bench and was the first to reach Wally and Felix. The familiar trio, arms waving high above their heads, led the tiny but mighty team off the floor. The small crowd of jubilant students and parents were on their feet shouting, "Hip, hip, hooray!"

At the locker room door, Manny stepped aside. The guys formed a single line to receive individual congratulations from Headmaster Jonathan Miller. "Nice job," he said, shaking each player's hand. "Keep up the good work and winning spirit for the school and our alumni fighting for us in this war."

Before Manny turned to go back onto the floor to gather up the equipment, he made eye contact with Felix. "My house in thirty minutes," he mouthed. "Tell Wally."

"You really put it to 'em," Manny said. He took another handful of Cracker Jack and passed the box to Wally. "From where I was sitting on the bench, I could hear comments from the crowd. Everyone was jeering because they said our school was a small, college-prep school with players who didn't know a thing about basketball. They thought beating us would be a piece of cake."

Manny took another swig from his bottle of root beer and continued praising his friends. He told Wally the opponent's player looked like a fool when he went up too quickly to block the winning basket.

Wally was six feet, one inch, the tallest and no doubt the best player on the team. He was the center. He had mastered a shot from outside the foul line that he had learned from his older brother, Carl. Carl had won a basketball scholarship to Ohio State University, but his college basketball career was on hold while he served in the army.

Felix was half an inch shorter. He was a menacing forward. Coach Pelley called him the team's sparkplug.

Manny and Felix had been shooting baskets together since Manny's father put up the hoop at the end of their driveway. Manny could see the hoop from his bedroom window. Felix's bedroom faced the driveway, too.

The two developed their own sign language. For as long as Manny could remember, they were able to stand at the window and talk to each other. One time, Manny's mother had called up to him from the foot of stairs and asked what he was doing.

"Talking to Felix," he answered.

"I didn't hear him come in," she responded.

"He didn't."

Manny then signed to Felix what had happened. Felix doubled up with laughter. "Shhhhh, don't tell," he motioned. And it had been their secret ever since.

Manny was Felix and Wally's greatest fan.

Manny started to get up from the table to walk to the icebox to get Wally another root beer when he remembered. "Hey, what time is it?"

"Just about 9:30 p.m.," Felix said, looking at his watch. "You got a problem?"

"I almost forgot to tell you," Manny said. He pulled the folded newspaper clipping from his wallet. "Did you guys see this?"

He memorized the sports desk's number before tossing the piece of paper on the table for Wally and Felix to read. They reached for it at the same time. "Read it aloud, Felix," Manny said. "I've got to make a telephone call. I'll be right back."

Manny was on the phone in the hallway between the dining room and kitchen. The other boys could hear him talking, but they couldn't understand what he was saying. Then silence. When he walked back into the room, he wasn't smiling.

"So what did they say about the dynamic college prep team beating the much bigger city team? Did they liken us to David and Goliath?"

"Not really," Manny said. He reached for the box of Cracker Jack. It was empty.

He got up and walked to the pantry to find a new box. He needed time. How could he tell them that this sports editor had said the University School was too small for any in-depth coverage? The Brew said the class C division didn't rank high enough for coverage. He would run the score of their games but not the details. He said no one cared about sports programs in the private schools.

"But it says right here in the paper—"

"I know. I know," Manny interrupted Felix. It wasn't their fault that the University School schedule didn't have them playing all the big city and county schools. "We'd beat most of 'em," Manny said. "Nobody, but nobody, has a tricky pump shot like Wally. He confuses every guard on every team we play."

"It's not fair," Wally said. He sounded and looked like Nora when she puckered her lips and wailed that everyone was being unfair making her go to bed before Manny.

Wally sat in the chair, staring into space. Then he shrugged his shoulders. "What the heck," he said, getting up from the table. "We should be used to it. Nobody cares about a little college-prep school. Besides, there's nothing we can do about it. Come on, let's go, Felix."

Felix got up to follow Wally. "Hey, wait," Manny said, following them into the hallway where they were putting on their coats and boots.

"What are we waiting for?" Felix said. "The sports editor told you we just aren't important enough."

As they walked down the porch steps, he could hear his two best friends making plans to meet to talk about strategy for the next game. Manny wasn't going to be included in that meeting.

Slowly, he shut the door. Being the team manager wasn't going to be enough to keep up his friendship with his Felix and Wally. And now his plan to be their greatest promoter by getting their game information in the newspaper wasn't going to happen.

I hate that sports editor, The Brew, he thought. But then he remembered Howard and how he wasn't a quitter. Manny would have to think of something.

Maybe we can play basketball incognito, he thought as he smiled.

CHAPTER 4

THE NEXT FEW DAYS WERE busy for everyone, but Manny had just enough time to put his plan into action.

As he waited for Felix and Wally to sit in chairs on either side of him, he looked straight ahead at the silver, cloth star that his mother had hung in the living room bay window. A group of mothers who had sons fighting in the war came up with the idea for the stars. About twelve inches in diameter, they were hung in the windows as a reminder to everyone. A silver star meant that someone in the family was serving overseas. A gold star hanging in the window announced that another young American had died fighting for his country.

Manny had counted seven silver stars in windows on his way home. He didn't see any gold stars. He prayed he never would.

"Hey, does your mom want me to take off my boots?" Felix yelled from the mudroom.

"She's not here. Are they wet?"

"No."

"Come on in and grab a root beer from the icebox for me, will ya, please?"

Felix put the brownish-yellow glass bottle in front of Manny. "Thanks. Sit here." Manny pointed to the chair on his right.

"Where's Wally?"

"He'll be—" Manny started when he heard the back door slam. "Speak of the devil."

"I didn't do it," Wally said, walking into the room, leaving behind a puddle of wet snow with each step he took.

"Hey, take off your boots. Mom will have a fit."

"Ooops, sorry, Mrs. Keefer, wherever you are."

"She's at the hospital."

"Did she make any chocolate chip cookies?" Wally asked as he hopped on his right stocking foot and pulled his boot off his left foot.

"No. My aunt Etta made oatmeal cookies." Manny pointed to the cookie jar. "Eat at your own risk."

Aunt Etta was Manny's favorite aunt, but she was a horrible cook. Manny thought all mothers and aunts were born with a code for how to bake, at the very least, chocolate cookies, but apparently, Aunt Etta had missed out.

Wally walked directly to the kitchen counter, picked up the lid, and dipped his hand into the jar, pulling out three cookies. He walked in his stocking feet into the dining room. He bit into one of the cookies just as he took a seat to Manny's left. "Hey, this is as hard as a rock!" he yelped. "I think I broke my tooth. Can you see a crack?" he asked, pointing to his front tooth.

Wally called Duncan, who was lying next to Manny's chair. The dog opened his eyes and looked at Wally but didn't move. "You can't fool Duncan, Wally." Manny laughed. "He doesn't eat Aunt Etta's cookies either."

Wally got up from the table and went into the kitchen, where he spit the cookie in his mouth into the sink. He threw the other two cookies into the wastepaper can.

When he was seated again at the table, Manny said, "Okay, let's talk basketball. What did you expect to get out of reading the results of the University School games in the daily newspaper?"

"Recognition," Wally said without a moment's hesitation. "We've got a good team and nobody knows it."

Felix nodded in agreement. "R-E-C-O-G-N-I-T-I-O-N. Recognition, recognition, sis, boom, bah." He spelled it out as he stood up to lead the cheer. Manny and Wally watched their friend march around the table.

Felix sat down again in his chair, looking surprised at his own emotional outburst. "And I thought it would be fun to see my name in the morning newspaper," he added sheepishly. "But, hey, it's not going to happen because we're not a big enough school for the newspaper to print anything more than the score."

Manny reached into his pocket and pulled out a clipping that he had carefully cut out of the morning newspaper. "Read the story with the headline 'New Team Wins Big.'"

After reading the three-paragraph story twice, Wally asked what was so important about that story. "So there's some new school in the area. So what? Big deal. They can't be very good. Maybe they're looking for teams to play. I'll ask Coach Ellis to call 'em up and ask to set up a game. Maybe we'll get some recognition in the newspaper."

"I wouldn't do that if I were you," Manny warned.

Manny explained that after The Brew had told him that the University School wasn't big enough for anything more than just printing the score, he started to wonder just how big or how unique a school would have to be for some recognition. He imagined a team that had a tall superstar supported by players who played together as team on the court and were best friends off the court. They knew each other so well they could predict each other's next move.

He imagined them being neighbors living on a street just like Elm Hill Drive, where he and Felix and Wally lived. That team became so real to him that the next night, he called The Brew to tell him about the new small Elmsdale High School that beat their opponents by more than twenty points.

"You mean there isn't any Elmsdale High School," Felix questioned, not understanding what Manny was saying.

"No, except in here." Manny pointed to his head.

"But it says there is, right here," Wally said, pointing to the newspaper article.

Manny explained he was a little bit scared when he first heard The Brew's voice on the telephone. But he decided to go forward and grew confident, his voice stronger with each word, especially when he could hear The Brew typing as fast as he could give him the information. The Brew was buying into it, falling for the story hook, line, and sinker.

Wally wasn't getting what Manny was saying. "You called this editor with information about a team that's in your head? Why?"

"A joke or, I don't know, maybe to prove a point. The Brew was so negative about our team. Said we weren't big enough or good enough. He acted like he knew everything. I thought I'd make something up, call him, and see what would happen. I really didn't think he'd print anything. But ..."

He pointed to the three paragraphs at the top of the page.

"Let's do it again tonight," Felix said. He always did enjoy a good joke, and he never hid the fact that he thought Manny was the cleverest person he knew.

"We can't," Manny said.

"Right. An editor won't fall for it again," Wally said. "Come on, Felix. I told my mom that I would be home early."

"No, that's not the problem," Manny said. He walked over to the icebox, grabbed another bottle of root beer, took a swig, and smacked his lips before continuing. "It's just that when I call him, I have to be prepared. We have to have names of players and names of the teams we play ready to give him."

Manny admitted that he was afraid last night that he had blown it. After giving him the information, The Brew got real nosey and asked a lot of questions. He wanted to know where the school was located, how many students went there, and who the coach was. Manny had dodged that question by muttering a name, Hamilton, for some reason. "I don't know why I said Hamilton," he told his friends.

"I do." Felix smiled. "We're studying Alexander Hamilton in Mrs. Pierce's civics class."

Manny hadn't thought of that, but he told Felix he was right.

"Not very smart, Keefer," Wally said. "There really is a Hamilton, Ohio, and it's not too far from Cincinnati."

"So what?" Felix questioned, irritated that Wally was so negative.

"I knew I was in even bigger trouble when The Brew asked me the name of the player with the highest points," Manny continued. "That's when I told him I had to go, my mother needed me. I told him he could write about the team or not. Then I hung up."

The three sat looking at each other, not saying a word. Wally broke the silence. "Can you believe this guy? He gives the imaginary Elmsdale High more press than the real University School. We deserve some recognition."

Before Manny could respond, Felix said, "Wally, you're missing the point. The University School deserves recognition. But for now, this editor, The Breeewwww, isn't going to give us any. So why not go along with Manny's joke? The joke is on The Brew giving press to a team that doesn't exist."

Manny grinned. He and Felix had always been on the same wavelength. Why not pull the wool over The Brew's eyes? They would be the only three people in the world who would know. The joke would be on The Brew.

But they had to promise not to tell anyone, Manny warned. Felix quickly agreed, but Wally didn't answer.

"Wally, are you in?" Manny asked.

"I don't know," Wally said. "I don't like this."

"I'm in. Cross my throat and hope to choke," Felix said.

"Wally?" Manny asked again.

Finally, he agreed.

"Say it," Felix demanded.

"Cross my throat and hope to choke."

"Great. Okay, Manny, when do we get started?"

Manny said they should meet after basketball practice the next day at Manny's house. The three friends locked hands and swore secrecy. "Only the phantom knows," Felix quipped.

Manny heard his friend, thought about it a second, and then said, "That's a good word. We'll be the Elmsdale High School Phantoms."

CHAPTER 5

MANNY HELPED MR. GLUTZ LOCK up after the grocery store closed. He had been helping out—bagging groceries and stocking shelves—ever since their son had enlisted in the navy. So far, this job hadn't interfered with his schoolwork or his time spent as the team manager.

As he hurried home, he worried that Mr. Glutz might need him more at the grocery. What if he had to give up his job as the team manager? That was all the more reason why this phantom basketball team was so important. He needed it to keep his friendship with Felix and Wally.

Manny hung up his coat and slid his boots under the bench in the mudroom before he walked into the dining room. His parents and Aunt Etta had already eaten and were carrying their dishes into the kitchen.

"Emanuel, I saved a bowl of my special soup for you. It's in the icebox," Aunt Etta said as she passed him at the doorway.

"Ahh, thanks, Aunt Etta, but I ate with Mrs. Glutz. She opened a can of Spam. I ate the whole thing by myself. I was going to bring it home, but I was so hungry."

Aunt Etta looked disappointed. His father gave him a knowing look, like it was okay that he missed the soup, since Aunt Etta had the reputation for being a terrible cook. But then, to Manny's surprise, his father said it was the best soup he had ever tasted.

"Did Aunt Etta make it—really?" Manny couldn't believe what he was hearing. He forgot Aunt Etta was standing there.

She either didn't hear or she ignored the question. "I got the idea for it when I was trying to think of something different to make on my night to cook. I took the leftover meats and beans and started putting them in the pot. I used the broth your mother had saved from the chicken we ate on Sunday."

"She named it World War II soup," Nora said. "You'd better have some before we eat it all."

"Maybe later," he said. "Hey, talking about food, you'll never guess what we got in the store today. It's called Oleo. Mr. Glutz says it's really just grease, but it comes with a yellow powder that you mix into it to make it look like butter."

Aunt Etta found the idea of Oleo amazing, but his mother said it sounded dreadful. His father said it was another sacrifice they all must make while their boys and girls were winning a war for us over there.

In unison, they all said, "These are not ordinary times."

Nora, who was sitting quietly with her head down, suddenly came alive. "I'm doing something important too," she said. "I'm collecting cans and other stuff that has metal in it."

Organizations across the country had heard their government's call for metal to make machines and guns for the war. Mrs. Blonde, Nora's second-grade teacher, had made a contest of it. Whoever collected the most pounds of scrap would win a prize. "I could win the most beautiful doll in the world," Nora swooned. "I have to win that doll."

Aunt Etta walked over to the trashcan and pulled out an empty can of peas. "Let me be the first to contribute to Nora's scrap drive. Before we're finished, we'll have bags and bags of cans. Just you watch."

Manny was surprised at how determined his little sister seemed to be about being the winner. "I'll ask customers at the grocery to save their cans for you," he promised. The grocery store was the center of the community these days as people stood in line waiting with their coupons to buy meat, sugar, and flour.

Manny was interrupted by the sound of footsteps on the front porch and then the doorbell. "Ah, that's our neighbors," Dad said. "I asked them to stop by around seven o'clock so we can talk about the air-raid practices."

Manny had forgotten about the neighborhood meeting. "Gosh, Dad, didn't I tell you that Wally and Felix were going to stop by tonight to ... ah ... to study?"

"I'm sure their parents will be here tonight, too. It'll be good for you boys to listen. Everyone has to know what to expect. The meeting shouldn't last that long. They can stay after to study."

Manny helped carry the dining room chairs into the living room and then carried everyone's coats upstairs before he sat down to listen to his father. Manny admired his father and hoped he would be just like him some day. Howard already was.

"A siren can be sounded at any time of the night," Dad said. "We will not have any warning. You must be prepared." Manny's father suggested that people hang thick, dark drapes in the windows of one room where the family spent a lot of time and keep them pulled at all times. The drapes would keep the light from escaping. "You may have to spend many hours in this room until the danger is over."

"Are you sure we'll know the sound?" Wally's dad asked.

Manny's father said there would be no doubt. The sound would be high-pitched and mournful. First, it would alert everyone to the pending danger. Then it would sound again when all was clear. "Remember everyone is responsible for making sure all their lights are out until the siren is turned off," he said.

"The government can't believe the enemy would bomb America," Felix's father said.

"We have several war plants nearby," Manny's father explained. "And what about the chemical plant down along the river? These are all sites that our enemy might want to wipe out. We have to make sure we're prepared."

As the formal meeting came to an end, Aunt Etta brought out a plate full of her oatmeal cookies. Mom asked if anyone would like a glass of Kool-Aid.

Manny looked at his father for the okay to leave the room. He then motioned to Wally and Felix to grab their chairs and follow him into the dining room. He closed the sliding door behind them and then opened it again, when he heard Duncan clawing at the wood. "Hurry up. Get in here," he said as Duncan meandered in.

Wally, Felix, and Manny huddled together at one end of the table. Duncan took his spot next to Manny's chair.

"Well?" Wally questioned.

Manny looked up from his notes and followed Wally's nod to the other end of the table where Nora was busy coloring. "What are you doing, Nora?" Manny asked.

"Coloring. I'm going to send my picture to Howard. I want to finish it tonight."

"Nora, do you think you could color someplace else, like your bedroom?"

"No."

"Why not? Felix and Wally and I have something important that we have to do."

"Why don't you go to your room then?"

"We could, but we need to look at this book," he said, holding up the atlas. "We all have to look at it at the same time and write things down. We need a table."

"I need the table, too" she said, never lifting her head to confront Manny eye to eye.

Manny looked at Felix and Wally. He motioned with his head for them to meet in the pantry. "Look, guys, she's not moving. There's not a chance in the world she'll go upstairs by herself. Besides, she's busy coloring. She won't pay any attention to what we're doing. She's in her own little world."

They filed back into the dining room and again huddled together at the end of the long, oak table. Manny whispered that the first thing they had to do was name the team players. First, they needed a name for the star center.

All three thought for a moment. Then Felix started. "I like the name Sidney."

"Sidney!" Wally almost shouted. He couldn't believe what he was hearing.

"Shhhhh," Manny said. He motioned toward Nora and the living room where their parents were still gathered.

"My sister named her cat Sidney," Wally whispered. "He's a sissy cat, afraid of his own shadow. And I know a girl named Sidney."

But Felix persisted. Sidney was his favorite uncle's name. And his uncle Sidney was big, tough, and could arm wrestle. Felix put his arm on the table and challenged Wally to a contest. They glared at each other. The muffled sounds of their parents talking in the front room filled the air.

"Okay, let's compromise," Manny whispered. "Let's shorten it to Syd and spell it with a *y*. S-Y-D. Okay?"

Wally said, "Okay. What's his last name?"

Manny had an answer for that. He had lain in bed the night before figuring out exactly what it should be. "Rachel. R-A-C-H-E-L," he said, surprising Wally and Felix with the quickness of his answer. His tone made it clear that there would be no further discussion of the last name.

"That sounds like a girl's name, too," Wally complained again loudly. Manny warned him to whisper. "This team is going to be a bunch of wimps. They'll play like girls. You got a favorite aunt Rachel?"

"No, it's a combination of the names of the other guys on the University School team: RAy Burns, CHuck Tanner, and Larry ELfers."

Felix wrote the name *SYD RACHEL* in big letters on the piece of paper in front of him. He slid the paper out in the middle of the table for Manny and Wally to see.

"Looks like a winner," Manny said just as the dining room door opened and his father appeared.

"Still hard at work, I see," his father said. "You must have some big school project. Is it a debate? I hear a lot of discussion going on."

Manny, Wally, and Felix all reached for the paper at the same time, ripping it in two and leaving one-half in Felix's hand and the other in Manny's hand.

"Ahh, right, Dad. Like, um, a debate exam."

His father nodded at the scrap of paper in Manny's hand. "Hope that wasn't something important that you have to write again." His tone let them know he didn't believe everything they were saying.

"No, just some notes," Manny said. He shoved his half of the paper into the atlas.

Felix shoved his half in his pocket and then changed the subject. "How did the meeting go, Mr. Keefer?"

Before he could answer, Manny's mother poked her head in the room and told Nora it was time to think about going to bed.

"Right on, Mom. That's a great idea," Manny said.

Nora gave him a look that could kill. "Just a little bit longer," she pleaded. "I want to finish my picture for Howard."

"Okay, but just fifteen more minutes. And Manny, I think you and Wally and Felix should wrap up what you're doing. Tomorrow is another day."

Manny got up to kiss her good-night. "We won't be long," he promised.

Wally waited until he heard Manny's parents start up the steps to go to bed before he said, "I think one of the players should be named Muehlenkamp."

"That name sounds familiar," Felix said.

"It should. We pass by the Muehlenkamp Funeral Home every day on our way to school," Wally explained.

"He'll be our player with the deadly shot from center court," Manny said.

Felix added that his identical twin brother would have a deadeye shot from the free-throw line. "Their names are Tim and Ted Muehlenkamp."

Manny liked the idea that it was Felix who suggested a player who was great from the free-throw line. He hoped Felix was remembering how good a free-thrower Manny was and how he made a difference to the team when they were a team. He wrote the names down on another piece of paper. "Three down. Two to go."

The three looked at the oak tabletop for inspiration. When he squinted, Manny could picture Syd, spelled with a *y,* Rachel moving the ball down the center of the hardwood table.

Felix broke the silence. "We have to have a Wynn. Because that's what the Elmsdale High Phantoms do, *win,"* he said. Manny added George Wynn to the list of names.

The cuckoo clock struck nine. "We've got to hurry, guys. Mom will call down any minute."

Silence.

"I want to have a player named Feldhouse," Nora piped up.

Manny, Felix, and Wally looked at each other. They had forgotten all about Nora.

"Who asked her?" Wally questioned.

Manny motioned for him to be quiet. "What made you think of the name Feldhouse?" he asked.

"My best friend's name is Susie Feldhouse. I love her name." Nora never lifted her eyes from her paper. She kept coloring.

Manny shrugged his shoulders and motioned for Wally and Felix to follow him into the kitchen.

"Do we have to use the name she wants?" Wally asked.

"I think we do. She'll never let up."

"Could she blow this for us?" Felix asked.

"Nah, she doesn't know what we're really doing. Let's name the last player Willie Feldhouse. That'll keep her quiet for sure."

The three walked back into the room. "Okay, Feldhouse it is. We'll use that name in our assignment. But don't mention this to anybody. Not even Aunt Etta or Susie Feldhouse."

"I won't."

"Cross your throat and hope to choke?"

"Promise."

Satisfied that she was now a part of this conspiracy, Nora quickly put her crayons in a box and gathered her papers together. She walked over to Manny and handed him the picture she'd drawn.

"What's this, Nora?" Manny asked. Felix and Wally jumped out of their chairs to get a better look.

Five bold stick figures dressed in red and yellow shorts and T-shirts stood on a dining room table. A big, blue ball was suspended in the white space above their heads. A black dog that looked like Duncan was sitting on the sidelines.

The three looked at it each other.

"What is this?" Manny asked again.

"Can't you tell, dummy? It's you, Wally, and Felix working on your assignment. Duncan's the cheerleader."

"Can I keep this, Nora?" Manny asked, folding it carefully so that it would fit in the atlas. She nodded her approval.

"Don't forget, Nora. Not a word about our assignment. It's our secret," Manny called after her.

"Promise. Cross my heart. Hope to croak."

Manny was about to correct her but then thought better of it. As soon as they heard her walking up the steps, Wally asked, "Are you sure she won't tell your mom?"

"What's to tell?"

"Yes, and she gave me an idea," Felix said. "We'll make Duncan our mascot. You know, the Elmsdale High Phantoms' mascot the Dunkin' Dog. Get it? We'll tell The Brew that we have a mascot just like President Roosevelt's dog. That'll get him."

Wally got up from his chair and headed for the mudroom to get his coat and boots.

"Hold on, one minute. The Phantoms have to have some opposition."

Manny held up the atlas, explaining they could use it to find names of small towns in Ohio.

Wally and Felix leaned over the table as Manny used his finger to go down a list of names in the book.

"Stop. Waynesville sounds good," Wally said.

Manny printed the name Waynesville at the top of a new sheet of paper.

Felix frowned. Manny asked, "What's the matter?"

"I don't think we should have the exact name of the town. What if the town really has a basketball team? We don't want to take too many chances. We already have Hamilton and that's a real town. Let's change the names a little, like, umm, Waynesburg."

"Good thinking, Felix." Next to the name "Waynesville," Manny put a dash and printed, "Waynesburg."

Once they got the idea, Manny had trouble keeping up. Wally

and Felix shouted out names in singsong fashion that sounded like a rallying cheer for the Phantoms.

Perrysburg—Berrysville.

Middletown—Middleburg.

Ottoville—Ottotown.

Reilly—

They were so involved with the name game that they didn't hear Manny's mother calling from the head of the stairs. "Emanuel, are you still downstairs? Are the boys still here?" Mom questioned.

"We're just finishing up. They're leaving right now."

Felix and Wally already had their coats on and were making their way out the back door. "See ya, Manny."

Manny tore all the papers that had any kind of writing on them into little pieces and tossed them into the wastepaper can. He started to fold the piece of paper with the list of opponents when he noticed the blank space next to Reilly.

"Reilly, breilly, treilly" he said aloud.

"Manny!"

"Coming, Mother." Quickly, he printed Riley, folded the paper, and stuck it in the atlas on the same page with Nora's drawing. He walked into the living room and shoved the book back into its space on the bookshelf, where it was immediately lost among the hundreds of books that lined the whole wall.

No one would ever think to look for information about a fantasy basketball team in an atlas.

CHAPTER 6

M ANNY CLOSED THE BEDROOM DOOR quietly behind him and tiptoed barefoot down the hallway past Nora's bedroom. Outside his parents' bedroom, he stopped, looked at the floor, and then stepped over the board that always creaked with any kind of pressure.

At the bottom of the stairs, he slid his feet, one at a time, into his slippers. The slapping of his slippers on the hardwood floor was the only sound in the cold, dark hallway. He peeked through the lead-glass window. The morning newspaper was lying in the snow about four feet from the front porch.

Quietly, he opened the door and then tiptoed onto the porch and down the wood steps to the paper. As he stooped down to pick up the bundle, his right slipper slid on the ice. He went crashing to the concrete.

He jumped up. No one had seen him. All the houses were pitch dark. The street light cast strange shadows in the yards that were covered with a light blanket of new snow.

Manny scooped up the paper with one hand and made his way back to the porch. He turned the knob of the front door. His hand slipped. The newspaper fell out from under his arm to the floor with a thud.

He tried the doorknob again. It wouldn't turn. Could it be frozen?

He tried again. Was it possible the door was locked? He couldn't believe it. His parents never locked the front door.

"Nora locked it," he said. "All the talk about war and the Japanese and raids scared her."

Now what? He pulled the collar of his robe up around his neck. He looked out onto the dark street. The temperature had to be in the twenties. The church clock bell pierced the icy air. Dong. Dong. Dong. Dong. Dong.

I can't wake up Mom and Dad, he thought.

He walked to the side of the porch and looked up at Felix's bedroom window. It was as dark as the winter morning.

If he could find stones hidden under the snow, he could reach Felix's window with one good toss. Felix would wake up when he heard the tat-tat sound. He always did in the summer.

Manny started to walk off the porch when movement behind the front door window caught his attention.

He peered through the glass. Nora was standing there in her long nightgown and robe. She was wiping her eyes. She held a broom in her right hand like it was a weapon. Duncan stood on guard at her side, his head tilted, ready to bark at any unfamiliar sound outside.

"Nora, open up. It's cold out here," Manny said in a low voice.

"Who is it?" She inched her way closer to the door.

"It's Manny. Hurry up."

"I can't see you," she said.

Manny pressed his face against the cold windowpane and crossed his eyes. "See? It's Manny. Hurry up, pleeeezzzze. I'm freeeeezzzzing."

Nora tripped over the broom handle as she made her way to the door. Manny danced from one foot to other to try to keep warm. Finally, after what seemed like an eternity to Manny, she opened the door.

31

Manny rushed in, hugging the newspaper as if it could keep him warm. "What are you doing up, Squirt?" he asked.

"I heard the floor squeak. And then I heard all kinds of strange noises. Maybe we are being invaded."

Suddenly Manny thought about how frightening it must be for children who heard adults talk about war and invading and sneak attacks and scary times.

"Hey, Squirt, I'm the one who made the floor squeak. There is no stranger in the house. You have to go back to bed. It's Saturday morning. It's too early to get up."

"I'm not tired. I want to be with you."

He looked at the newspaper in his hand and walked toward the kitchen. Nora followed. He turned on the overhead light and pulled the sports section from the paper.

"I'm cold," Nora cried. She wrapped her arms around herself to keep warm. She looked as cold as he felt. He explained there was no heat in the house, but if she went back to bed, she would be warm under the blankets."

"No." She had that look on her face that told Manny she wasn't going to budge. He scanned the headlines on the front of the sports page. He didn't see Elmsdale High School. Hadn't The Brew written anything about the fabulous Phantom Five?

"Maaannnnnyyyy, I'm cold."

Manny gave up. He put the paper on the table and headed to the door leading to the basement. Nora shadowed him. He told her to stay upstairs, but she refused. "Okay, but I'm warning you it'll be tough going down the steps. And you won't like it down there one bit. There might be bugs crawling around."

"I don't care. I'm going with you."

Manny opened the door to the dark hole below. He used his left hand to feel the stucco wall. His right hand held on to the wood railing.

Nora held onto the flannel belt on his bathrobe with one hand and the railing with the other.

Slowly, they inched their way down one uneven, narrow, wood step after another. It seemed forever before Manny felt the concrete floor.

"Wait here," he said. "I'll turn on the light."

His slippers flapped against the floor as he made his way into the room. Manny hadn't been in the cellar for a long time. He had forgotten how low the ceiling was. Or maybe he had grown that much taller. Or maybe it was because it was so dark. He bent his head and shoulders and put his right arm out in front of him, feeling for the string to the bare light bulb.

Suddenly, out of nowhere, something moved across his face. He reared back. "Whooaaa!"

Nora cried out, "Manny!"

"Shhh," he said. "It was just the light cord." He pulled it and the light from the bulb cast eerie shadows in the room. But he could see well enough to find his way to the middle room, where he pulled the cord to another ceiling bulb.

Nora was on his heels. "Who's over there?" she shouted.

Manny gasped. He looked to his right and squinted his eyes so he could see better. Forms that were taller and wider than him lunged out at them, suspended in the air. Manny stood as quiet as a mouse. He didn't breathe. He waited. Nothing happened. The forms didn't move.

Then he knew.

"Ahh, that's nothing, Nora," he said. "That's just Mom's wash hanging on the line to dry."

Manny looked ahead to another dark room.

"I want to go back. I'm afraid," Nora whined.

"Okay. But you'll have to go back by yourself. I can't stop now."

Manny moved cautiously until he could see the old iron furnace that sat proudly in the most remote room of their house. He grabbed the bucket that Dad always kept next to the furnace. He opened the door to an even smaller room where dark coal was stored in a mound. Using the shovel that was leaning against the wall, he filled the bucket and then carried it to the furnace. He opened the heavy, iron door and peered inside. The coals glowed in the dark. He poured the new coal on top, closed the door, and repeated the process four times.

He was getting ready to fill another bucket when he heard Nora talking to their father.

"Manny, are you in there? Good morning. You're up early for a Saturday," Dad said while walking into the room. He opened the door to the furnace. The new coal was already burning. "Nice work. Looks like you're ready to take over Howard's job. Thanks. Now hurry upstairs. Your mother has breakfast started. I think she's fixing your favorite: cinnamon toast."

Nora was already sitting at the kitchen table. The newspaper was lying in front of her. He looked over at his mother. She was standing at the stove with her back to them. He grabbed the sports section and said, "Morning, Mom. What's for breakfast?"

"Give that back!" Nora shouted. "Mom, he took the paper I'm reading."

Nora persisted. "I want to read about Elmsdale High School!" she shouted.

"Who?" Mom asked.

Manny couldn't believe his ears. He dropped the paper in front of Nora. Anything to keep her quiet. He walked over to the icebox and poured himself a glass of milk, then casually returned to the table where he stood behind Nora and tried to read the newspaper over her shoulder.

He saw what he was looking for in the right-hand corner, next to an advertisement for a box of fresh cigars.

"Elmsdale High Wins Again," the bold headline shouted out at him.

Manny pulled a chair close to Nora, sat down, and started to read.

Syd Rachel, basketball find of the year, led the scoring with 23 points as Elmsdale High School walloped Waynesburg Township 59–23 last night in the winner's gym. It marked the third cage game in which the winning school has ever competed and its third successive victory.

Paced by Rachel, but with George Wynn and Ted Muehlenkamp hitting the hoop often, Elmsdale went ahead early and led throughout. Center Ackerman looked good for Waynesburg.

"He bought the whole thing," Manny said aloud, forgetting where he was.

"Who did? Who bought what, dear?" his mother asked. She set a plate piled with five pieces of toast, dripping with butter, sugar, and cinnamon, in front of him.

Manny bit into a piece. "Yuck!" he yelled, spitting the toast into his napkin.

"Dear, what's the matter?"

"This doesn't taste like cinnamon toast," he said. Before he could stop himself, he asked, "Did Aunt Etta make this?"

"I did not," Etta said, suddenly defensive.

His mother looked at him, shocked. Then she explained the difference in taste might be that she used Oleo. "You'll just have to acquire a taste for it," she said.

Before Manny could respond, Nora said, "Look at this, Manny."

She was pointing to the box score for the Elmsdale game. "There's Susie Feldhouse's name. What do these numbers mean?"

Aunt Etta was surprised that Nora was reading the sports page. She looked over Nora's shoulder to see what she was pointing at.

"I'm reading this story. That's Manny's team," Nora said. Manny squeezed her knee under the table. She yelped. "Hey, stop that. Mom, Manny is—"

"Children, will you please stop? Manny, didn't Mr. Glutz want you at the grocery store a little early this morning? You'd better hurry." She reminded Nora and Aunt Etta they had a lot of things to do that day, including finishing the care package for Howard. She asked Nora about the picture she was drawing for her brother.

"I gave it to Manny." She gave Manny one of her looks that could kill. "Where is it?" she snapped.

"Um, I don't have—"

"You do," Nora wailed. "It's my picture of your team."

"Oh yes, for our assignment. Gosh, Nora, I took that to school. I didn't know you wanted it back."

Aunt Etta, in an attempt to calm the waters, suggested Nora draw another picture. "You're such a good little artist, I'm sure you can do another one quickly."

Nora liked that idea and got up from her chair to go find paper and crayons. Manny followed her. He had to warn her not to talk about the Elmsdale team.

When they were far enough away from the kitchen, he stopped her. "Nora, you must promise not to mention Elmsdale High to Mom or Dad or Aunt Etta or anybody. It's a secret," he said quietly as they walked up the steps.

"Mommy said I shouldn't keep secrets."

"This is different. You, Wally, Felix, and I know the same thing. It's something confidential, not really a secret. And we're not going to keep it quiet forever. In fact, we'll let you tell everybody when we're ready."

Nora liked the idea of keeping a secret with Manny and his friends. She stopped in front of her bedroom door and whispered to Manny, "Cross my throat and hope to choke."

CHAPTER 7

MANNY CHECKED HIS WATCH. HE had ten minutes to get to Glutz's Grocery. He'd have to cut through Mr. Brewster's backyard.

A three-inch blanket of new snow covered the five inches that had fallen a couple of days ago. Mr. Brewster would see footprints and know that someone used his yard as a shortcut. He would see footprints, but he wouldn't know they were Manny's.

And he surely wasn't up yet. It wasn't even nine o'clock. Mr. Brewster stayed up until the wee hours of the morning. Sometimes, when Manny stayed up past midnight to cram for a test, he would see a light coming from a first-floor room in the three-story brick house that stood in the middle of his block.

He wondered what Mr. Brewster was doing at that time when most of the neighbors were asleep. But he wasn't about to ask him. No one in the neighborhood knew Mr. Brewster very well. No one liked him.

Manny thought Mr. Brewster was very mysterious. He was tall and thin. He had a full, salt-and-pepper beard. He always wore a cap pulled down to his eyes.

He never talked to anyone. He was always crabby, and even more crabby since his wife died last year.

Last summer, Mr. Brewster made playing ball in the street impossible. "Haven't you any better place to go?" he would yell.

He sat in a rocking chair at the front of the porch that wrapped around both sides of the house. The creaking sound of the rocker moving back and forth, back and forth, could be heard out on the street. He was just waiting for someone to make a mistake.

One day, it happened. A fly ball fell in his yard. He jumped off the porch, scooped it up as quickly as a professional shortstop, and took it into his house, slamming the door behind him.

They never got the ball back. But last Halloween, Manny and Felix got even. Quietly, they carried a garbage can onto his porch, tilted it against his front door, rang the doorbell, and then ran as fast as they could, hiding behind bushes in the yard next door.

From their hiding place, they could see his face when he opened the door and all the garbage spilled into his front hall. His face looked as if it was about to explode. Mr. Brewster almost fell over the garbage as he rushed out onto the porch and into his yard. He came very close to where they were hiding. Manny didn't breathe for about a minute.

Mr. Brewster looked up and down the street, and then stormed back into the house. Manny hadn't seen him at all in the past month. Maybe he wasn't living in the house anymore. Maybe he wasn't even living.

Manny walked as quickly as he could through the deep snow. He was almost to the fence at the back of the yard when he heard Mr. Brewster call his name.

"Emanuel Keefer. Is that you?"

Manny stopped in his tracks. Just one leap and he'd be over the fence and in the Johnson's yard. Mr. Brewster couldn't yell at him then.

"Yes," he said. He turned slowly.

"Where do you think you're going, Emanuel?"

"Glutz's Grocery. I work there. I bag groceries for them since their son got called to the war."

"Are you late? Is that why you're cutting through my yard?"

"Yes, sir, I am."

This was getting to be ridiculous, Manny thought. He certainly wasn't hurting any of his grass, because it was covered with snow. He knew better than to walk on the Brewster property any other time of the year. And what was it to Mr. Brewster anyway? No skin off his nose if Manny didn't get to work on time.

"See that you never do it again. Learn how to use your time better. You want to be a responsible adult, don't you?"

Spare me the lecture, Manny thought, but he said, "Yes, sir, I do. Just like my brother Howard. He is a US Marine in the South Pacific. He enlisted."

Mr. Brewster mumbled something Manny couldn't hear before he turned to go back into his house.

Manny was ready to cross the fence when Mr. Brewster called to him again. "You tell your sister that I've got quite a few cans saved for her and some other metal things. She can come over and get them any time she wants."

Manny couldn't believe what he was hearing. Was he talking about Nora? He walked back to face Mr. Brewster.

"What does Nora want the cans for? And why would she ask you?" Manny couldn't believe he was that blunt. But he couldn't picture Nora asking Mr. Brewster for anything. She was afraid of him. Manny had told her the Brewster house was haunted.

"She came to visit me one day last week. She's wants to win the scrap drive at school. She wants to win the doll. I told her I'd see what I had around the house. Anything wrong with that?"

"Mmmm, no, sir. Nothing at all. I'll tell her," he said taking off in a run.

Manny's watch showed 9:05 when he got to the grocery. "Good morning, Mrs. Glutz," he said as he passed Mrs. Glutz standing at the cash register. "I'm sorry I'm late."

"Good morning," she called after him. "Are you ready for a big day? Everyone will have their coupons for flour, sugar, and of course, cigarettes today."

Mr. Glutz was standing at the butcher's table cutting the excess fat off a piece of beef. Mrs. Miracle was standing at the meat counter with a list in her hand.

"Morning, Mr. Glutz," Manny said.

He walked to the corner where he kept the pole that he used to roll the green-and-gray awning over the front windows. His first chore of the day was to roll the awning down to keep the sun from shining in the store. His last chore was to roll it up again.

During the dreary days of winter, Manny didn't see much point in rolling the awning down, but it was a daily ritual that went into running the grocery store. The Glutz family had operated the neighborhood grocery for forty years.

After Manny finished the chore, he made his way to the back of the store. Customers were filling carts, the wheels squeaking on the uneven wooden floor, as they walked down the narrow aisles.

"Did you hear anything from your son?" Manny asked Mr. Glutz. He leaned the pole against the wall and grabbed his white apron from the hook.

Everyone in the store heard the question. They stopped to listen to the answer.

"A letter was waiting for us when we got home last night," Mr. Glutz said. He enjoyed the audience and talked a little louder so those in the front could hear.

"He wrote his mother and me that the weather is very warm. He said the food is usually good, but sometimes it seems as though the stew is seasoned with red ants."

Mrs. Carter, who was somewhere between the boxes of cereal and cans of vegetables, joined in the conversation.

Manny listened to the adults talking. He started to fill a cart with things that Josephine Winters had ordered over the telephone. She had just had twin boys. Her husband was in the army. She was living with her husband's parents just two blocks from the grocery store. That would be a short distance to pull the wagon, even though her order would fill at least eight bags. He might have to make two trips.

Manny wondered when his family would get a letter from Howard. It seemed like forever since he had written to them. He was being reassigned. He said he would send his new address as soon as he could. But that had been weeks ago.

Manny had so many things to tell him, especially about the Elmsdale High School team. He had five newspaper clippings stashed away in the box under his bed. Each article was a little longer than the other.

He wished he could tell Howard in person what was going on. Manny could see Howard throwing his head back, laughing his laugh that seemed to come from the bottom of his stomach. "That's a good one on The Brew," he'd say.

The next best thing to telling Howard in person would be to write it. But he had to make sure he had the correct address. He had only one set of clippings. He couldn't afford to lose them in the mail.

The Brew was taking a real interest in the Elmsdale Phantoms. He always came to the telephone immediately to personally take the information from Manny. Manny could hear The Brew typing as fast as Manny talked.

He was getting very nosey, however. He'd ask lots of questions. Why did the Phantoms play in their own gym? Why was it always the same referee? Who was the coach? And why did they always play such small schools that no one had heard of? And always, why had he never heard of the Elmsdale school before?

So far, Manny had been lucky and hadn't had to answer all the questions. Manny got the feeling The Brew was suspicious but didn't really want to know for sure. When Manny was vague or said, "Sir, I've got to run, my mother needs me," he would not push it. An account of the Elmsdale High School game would be printed under a bold headline in the morning newspaper.

Of course, Manny would have to swear Howard to secrecy. Promise? He would ask in a letter. Cross my throat and hope to choke, Howard would write back.

Howard would be no problem. Nora was something else. Manny still wasn't confident that Nora wouldn't spill the beans. But she was so busy trying to find scrap to win that silly doll. And besides, Manny was beginning to think that at least he should tell Dad and Aunt Etta. They'd get a good laugh out of it, just like Howard would when he wrote to him.

Thinking about Aunt Etta reminded Manny that he must remember to tell Howard that she had created her own soup and even Dad thought it was delicious. Manny thought it was good, too. He had sneaked into the kitchen when everyone else was gathered around the radio, listening to President Roosevelt's fireside chats. Duncan had followed him. Manny took one spoonful. He tried another and another and probably would have eaten it all, if Duncan hadn't looked like he would bark if he didn't get a share. Manny couldn't forget to tell Howard they called it Aunt Etta's World War II soup.

Manny was busy at the store the entire morning. He stocked shelves with cans of peas, corn, and green beans. Mrs. Dawson dropped a jar of pickles. Glass splattered everywhere. Manny cleaned it up first with a broom and then a rag mop. He made two deliveries: one to the Millers' house on Barry Lane and another to the Winters' house on Betula Lane. He was invited in to meet the twins. He'd never seen identical twins before in his life. Manny smiled when he thought of the Muehlenkamp twins, Ted and Tim, who played for the Elmsdale High Phantoms.

Mr. Miller and Mrs. Winters each gave him a quarter. He was saving his money to buy a birthday present for his brother. He saw a fine wood carved pipe in the Cigar Store on Twelfth Street that he knew Howard would like. It was expensive, though—$8.95. Manny didn't know if he would have enough money in time to buy it for Howard's May birthday.

"What kind of sandwich will it be today?" Mr. Glutz asked when he got back to the store about one o'clock.

Manny looked through the glass meat counter, taking in all the hunks of veal and pork and beef before pointing to the baloney and the ham. He then asked for a piece of Swiss cheese.

"Don't tell me. Light with mustard and *no* oleo." Mr. Glutz chuckled.

Manny sat on the chair behind the counter, his sandwich in one hand and a bottle of root beer in the other. Mr. Glutz stayed behind the meat counter to help Andy Meshman, whose wife usually did the shopping. Obviously uncomfortable with the situation, he handed Mr. Glutz a coupon booklet. "Alice says we have enough to buy some nice minute steaks for Sunday night dinner."

Mr. Glutz counted the coupons. "She's right. Would you like to point out the ones you like?"

"You pick what you think is the best," he said. "I just can't get used to shopping with coupons."

"Nothing is the same anymore, Andy. We just have to deal with it the best we can," Mr. Glutz said.

As the two men stood at the meat counter, their conversation turned to high school basketball. The Glutzes had been to the University School game the night before. "Good, scrappy, little team they got this year. Mr. Glutz pointed to Manny, who nodded his head. "Manny is the team's manager."

"They're scrappy, but they're just not big enough to be any kind of challenge for the bigger schools," Mr. Meshman said. "It'll be the usual—Walnut Hills High and Withrow—in the city tournament. They're always the big guns."

"There's another team—a small team—that seems to be coming on strong," a man next to Mr. Meshman said. Manny had never seen him before. "It's a new school. Ellsdale or Ellisale or something like that from out near Hamilton. The team hasn't lost a game."

"Never heard of 'em," Mr. Glutz said, putting the package of wrapped minute steaks on top of the counter. "Anything else, Andy?"

"Not today." He dropped the meat in his cart and turned to the stranger. "I've read about that Ellssdale team."

"Elmsdale," Manny corrected him.

"Seems to be a one-man team," the stranger continued. "There's this one kid, Bill or Jim Ratchell, who averages twenty points a game."

"His name is Syd, spelled with a *y,* Rachel," Manny said, walking over to the two men.

Mr. Glutz was surprised at how much Manny seemed to know about this new team. What had he heard about the team? Had he seen them play? And what about their star player?

Manny ignored all of the questions except one. "I hear that the Rachel player is not that good."

"Who says that?" the stranger asked. "The night I saw him play, he looked great. He's got a great outside shot."

Manny couldn't believe it. This was too good to be true. Wait until he told Wally and Felix. They wouldn't believe him.

"You actually saw him play?" Manny acted shocked and impressed. "You saw the great Syd with a *y* Rachel? Where did you see him play?"

The man looked at Manny, tilted his head just like Duncan did so often, and thought for a moment. "You know, I can't remember. I see so many games these days. As The Brew says, 'We must support our youth and their teams.' But I know this Rachel kid is a good, big, strong player. He's a definite for the city all-star team."

CHAPTER 8

Manny, Felix, Wally, and Nora huddled at one end of the long, oak, dining room table, planning the strategy for the next Elmsdale High game.

First question: how many points would Syd Rachel make in this game? Manny waited with his pencil and pad to take notes that he would use when he called The Brew.

Felix suggested twenty points.

"Oh no. Sounds like he's in a slump," Manny said. "Who's going to pick up the slack? One of the Muehlenkamp twins?"

"I want Feldhouse," said Nora, who had been sitting quietly at the corner of the table in the far end of the room. "Let him do something."

Wally and Felix, who were concentrating on deciding the points for each Phantom, looked up and turned to where Nora was sitting. They turned to Manny with looks that pleaded with him to do something about Nora. Manny shrugged his shoulders. What could he do?

"Okay, Nora, we'll let Feldhouse make a lot of baskets in this game."

Manny and Felix went down the list of players, deciding exactly how many field goals and free-throw shots each had.

Felix looked at the irregularly shaped box Manny had drawn on the notepaper. At the top of the page was printed, "Field Goals, Free

Throws, and Total Points." He added the points. "That's sixteen field goals for thirty-two points and fourteen free throws for forty-six points. How much did we say Elmsdale had?"

"Forty-three points."

"Better take a basket away from Tim Muehlenkamp and a free throw from Feldhouse," Felix said.

"No, not Feldhouse," Nora whined.

"Okay, okay," Felix said. "Give me the pencil, Manny. I'll erase one of those free throws from Wynn's score."

Satisfied that the number of points scored by the Phantoms added up to forty-three, Manny was ready with the next problem they needed to discuss. "Okay—" he began.

"I don't like it," Wally interrupted. Felix, Manny, and Nora all looked at him. "I'm starting to feel funny about this. That guy the other day at the grocery store talking about Elmsdale High like it's a team or something. That's weird. I feel like, I don't know, like we're picking somebody's pocket."

"Are you serious?" Manny asked. "This is fun. Nobody's getting hurt. The joke's on The Brew. He deserves it. And you said so too. He thinks he knows everything, but he won't give ink to the University School team. Have you seen any write-ups? But you guys have won some good games, soundly beating bigger schools."

Felix picked up on the idea that no one was getting hurt by their joke. Manny asked if the Elmsdale Phantoms should stop playing in midseason. How could they explain that?

"Nah, we can't do that, I guess," Wally said.

Manny waited for Wally to continue, but he didn't. "So are we okay with it?" Manny asked. "It's getting late. I've got to call in the game results to The Brew."

Manny turned the notebook pages to where he had written the names of the opposing teams. "Okay, the Phantoms play Riley High this week." He grabbed his notes and went into the hallway to make the call. Wally, Felix, and Nora followed.

Using one hand to hold the phone, he used the other to pump an imaginary basket. "That's two more," he mouthed to the other three just as someone answered the phone.

"Hello, this is the stringer for Elmsdale High," he said, regaining his composure. "Is The Brew there to take the information on another win for the Elmsdale Phantoms?" He winked at Nora as he waited for The Brew to come to the phone.

"Good evening, sir. This is the stringer for Elmsdale High. I'm sure it's not a surprise. We had another win." Manny was enjoying every minute of the conversation and played it up to the hilt.

"That's right, sir, Elmsdale's lead at the half was twenty-three to twelve. Syd, that's spelled with a *y*, as you well know, Rachel had twenty points tonight. A little low for our star, I know, but Feldhouse picked up where Rachel left off with eleven points."

He paused. He could hear The Brew typing as he talked. Manny smiled broadly at Nora.

"I'm sorry, I didn't catch what you said, sir."

His smile turned to a frown. "What's that? Why have you never heard of the Elmsdale Phantoms before? I thought I told you we are a new school. What's that? How did a school get enough money to build a new gym during wartime? I thought I told you how. What's that? Where did we get the money for a gym?"

He shrugged his shoulders and looked at Felix. Wally already was back in the dining room.

"Help," he mouthed.

"Sir, can you hear me?" he whispered. "I can't hear you. We have a terrible connection. I'll call you right back."

Manny slammed the phone down and stood frozen against the wall.

"Whew, that was close. Come on. Let's huddle. We need to make some decisions."

Felix, who thought all was going well and was enjoying watching Manny give the information, wanted to know what happened so quickly. What did The Brew want to know?

"He wants to know where our school got the money to build a gym. Think. Where'd we get it? I promised I'd call him right back."

"Are you really calling him back?" Wally couldn't believe it. "Man, this is a sign. I say we forget the whole thing. This guy knows something is up."

For the first time since they began this spoof, Felix agreed with Wally. "The Brew knows something's fishy."

"No, he doesn't," Manny protested. "He'll think something's fishy if I don't call him back. Come on, you guys. We can't stop now. Pretend it's a timeout, the fourth quarter, one minute to go. We're down by three. Felix, I mean Tim Muehlenkamp, is at the free-throw line. What do we do?"

The four sat in silence. The bobbing bird in the cuckoo clock heralded nine o'clock.

"Time's running out. I must make the telephone call if I'm ever going to make it. Should I, or should I not? Does Tim Muehlenkamp sink his second free throw or aim for the rim to give Rachel a chance to dunk it for two points?"

Again, silence.

"Wait. I know what I'll tell him," Manny said with a sudden flash of inspiration. "I'll tell him that our science teacher donated the money. He always wanted to play basketball when he was a kid, but his school didn't have a gym."

"That's great, Manny. But where did he get the money?" Felix asked. "From his aunt Tilly who just died?"

Wally threw up his hands in disgust. "This is ridiculous. Is Aunt Tilly married to Uncle Sidney? You guys are weird. I'm out of here."

Felix and Manny watched Wally get up and walk toward the back door. Nora hung her head. She was about to cry.

"Wally, wait a minute," Manny called after him. "Let me ask you one question. What's the worst thing that could happen?"

He thought for a moment. "I guess they just wouldn't print the score."

"Right. And what's it to us? No skin off our noses. Nobody knows. We're not going to get detention or be confined to our rooms."

Felix, who always supported Manny, saw the logic in this. He pleaded with Wally. "Why not? Nobody gets hurt. We owe it to Syd with a y Rachel and the boys."

Nora, who had been sitting with her head down, suddenly jumped to her feet. Tears ran down her cheeks. "I quit," she said. "I don't like this game anymore. I'm going to tell Mommy and Daddy and Aunt Etta and Susie Feldhouse."

"No," Wally, Felix, and Manny said in unison.

Manny grabbed for her arm. "Wait, Nora. You can't quit. You promised. We're just talking. Nothing will happen."

Wally hesitated. "Right, Nora. No problem. We're just talking."

No one said a word. The only sounds in the room were the tick, tick of the clock and Nora's sniffling.

"Well, what do we do?" Manny asked.

They all looked at Wally. "Ahh, go ahead. I guess we can't quit now." Then he looked at Nora. "Is that okay?" he asked. "If we don't quit, you won't tell anybody. Right?"

She shook her head. "Cross my throat, hope to choke," she whispered.

Manny jumped up from the table and headed for the telephone. He looked back at Nora. Somehow, she had turned off her tears just like she would a water faucet. She was all smiles.

Wally, Felix, and Nora waited patiently for Manny. "Well?" Felix asked when he returned to the room.

"He bought the whole story."

"Yes!" Felix gave Wally the high sign just like they did when Wally sank a long one for two points.

"And he thanked me for calling him back before his deadline."

"Good. Now, I've got to get going," Wally said. Felix was right behind him.

"The Brew did want one more thing."

Felix and Wally stopped in their tracks. They turned and looked at Manny. "He wants to know if Syd Rachel is playing in the city all-star game in two weeks." Before Wally or Felix could respond, Manny added, "I told him yes."

Wally looked at Felix. Felix shrugged his shoulders. "But how can Rachel play. He's—"

Before Wally could finish, Manny continued. "Then The Brew asked me for a photograph of Rachel. I told him I'd get it to him next week."

"You're crazy!" Wally exclaimed. "In case you don't remember, Manny, there is no Syd Rachel."

"What are we going to do?" Felix wanted to know.

"I'm not sure. But I'll think of something by the time we meet again at the University School team practice on Sunday."

CHAPTER 9

F IVE MINUTES AFTER HE TURNED off the lamp that was sitting on the small table next to his bed, burrowed under his feather blankets, and rested his head on the pillow, Manny was sound asleep, dreaming about basketball.

A man dressed like a referee in black and white stripes was staring down at him as they stood midcourt in the University School gym. The stream rolling out of the top of his head and ears masked the man's face.

"I don't get it, Syd, that's with a *y*, Rachel. I've made you a basketball star and you can't even hit the side of the barn," the man said while pointing a finger in Manny's face. "What is it with you? You're making me the laughingstock of the community. Look at them."

Manny looked over at the bleachers where Wally, Felix, Nora, and Howard were booing loudly. "Bench him, Coach. He's no good!" Howard was yelling at the top of his lungs.

"But I'm not Syd with a *y* Rachel!" he cried. "I'm Manny Keefer. Can't you see? There is no Syd spelled with a *y* Rachel."

"That's not what your skin says."

Shocked, Manny looked at his hands. All he could see was Syd with a *y* Rachel tattooed all over skin that was as rough as a crocodile's. He was no taller than Nora. And his hands were webbed like a duck's feet.

Manny looked up again at the man. This time he saw "The Brew" printed in big red letters across the left breast pocket of his striped uniform.

Before Manny could answer, he was awakened by the loud eerie sound of a horn, then a knock on his door. "Manny, Manny. It's Dad. We're having an air-raid practice. Do you hear me? Are you awake?"

Just as Manny turned on his bedside lamp, his father opened the bedroom door. "No, no, don't turn on the light. That's exactly what not to do."

"Oops, sorry," Manny said, quickly reaching for the light switch.

"That's all right, son. Everyone else on the street will probably turn on their lights when they hear the siren, too. That's why we have drills. I need your help. We have to walk down the street and make sure everyone's house is pitch dark."

Manny jumped out of bed and dressed quickly. The clock on his dresser said it was four o'clock. He had set the alarm for five. He wanted to get the morning newspaper and read it before everybody else got up.

His father was waiting for him at the foot of the stairs. He plopped a hard, gray helmet on Manny's head. It was too big and slipped over his right eye.

"You have to adjust the chin strap," his father said, trying not to smile. "Here. Put this arm band on. It means you're officially helping me. Take this flashlight. Keep it pointed to the ground, and only turn it on when you need it."

Manny took his coat from the hall hook and followed his father out into the dark, cold night. At the end of the walkway, his father pointed down the street. "You take that side of the street. I'll take this side. If anyone has a light on, go up to the door and knock loudly. Call to them by name so they aren't frightened."

"What do I say?"

"Tell them it's not a raid, only a drill. They must keep their houses dark. If they have to get up, tell them to go to the room where they have dark curtains. They can turn on a light in that room because the curtains hide the light."

"It's spooky out here, Dad."

"I know. We have to practice. Whenever our government officials see suspicious planes in the area, they will sound the air-raid siren. We all must remember to keep the lights off after the siren sounds and until the all-clear siren is blown. If our enemies should try to bomb us, they will not know where the city is. Without lights, the city is an empty pit from the air."

The thought that the enemy might bomb them shot chills down Manny's spine. He shivered, but it wasn't the subfreezing temperatures that made him cold.

The high-pitched, eerie sound of the siren hurt his ears. Finally, it stopped. He was unnerved. It was so dark. The moon was hiding behind thick, gray clouds. He couldn't move. He stood for a second, listening to the snow crunching under his father's boots as he made his way down the street.

"Hurry, Manny," his father called back to him. "Start checking the houses."

Manny looked up and down the street as far as he could see. A light shining through the window, illuminating the snow, came from only one house.

"Ahh, no," he said to no one but himself. "It's Mr. Brewster's house."

Slowly, he made his way across the street. He turned on his flashlight only when he thought he was close to the curb. But he was too late. He tripped, falling forward before he could catch himself. His flashlight slid across the ice, stopping in the snow. Quickly, he jumped up, only to lose his balance again on the icy sidewalk. He caught himself this time before he fell.

"Of course, Mr. Brewster's sidewalk is the only one on the street that hasn't been shoveled," he said aloud. Talking to himself gave him the courage he needed to keep moving. He couldn't see or hear his father anywhere.

Manny walked up the sidewalk to Mr. Brewster's house and stood outside the lighted window. "Mr. Brewster. Mr. Brewster. Mr. Brewster." He called a little louder each time.

"Well, that's not going to work, Emanuel Keefer," he said sternly to himself again, sounding like Mr. Brewster did when he called his name. He made his way up to the wooden porch that was even more slippery than the sidewalk. "This is like a skating rink."

He used his flashlight to find the button for the doorbell. He pushed it. No sound. He tried again. Still nothing. He took off his gloves and started to knock on the door. He knocked gently at first, but it didn't take long before he was pounding as hard as he could.

"He's got to be deaf," he said, reaching for the doorknob as a last-ditch effort. "I bet I'm at the only house in the whole city that still has a light on."

To his surprise, and dismay, the knob turned. "Oh no! Now I've gotta go in." Slowly, he pushed the door open. "Mr. Brewster. Mr. Brewster. Please answer me."

The door opened into a huge entry hall with a ten-foot ceiling and doorways on either side that led to other rooms. Straight ahead was a steep, narrow staircase. A narrow hallway next to the steps seemed to lead to nowhere. The light was coming from the room on Manny's left. "Mr. Brewster, are you in there?"

Keeping the flashlight up to his face so Mr. Brewster would know who it was and wouldn't shoot if he had a gun pointed at the doorway, Manny made his way into the room.

Mr. Brewster was sitting in the captain's chair at the dining room table. His head was resting on his chest. For a second, Manny thought he might be dead. But then he saw Mr. Brewster's plaid flannel shirt move ever so slightly as he breathed in and out.

The table in front of him was cluttered with newspaper clippings with bold headlines. "Brewster Is Rookie Pitcher of the Year." "Brewster Throws Three-Hitter." "Brewster Wins Another."

Manny picked up one clipping and looked at the young, smiling face in the baseball cap. He looked at the old man sleeping at the end of the table. "Is that Mr. Brewster?" Manny questioned aloud.

When he was closer to the table, other headlines told another story. "Star Pitcher's Son Killed in Action." "Brewster Accepts Purple Heart for His Son."

Manny picked up the clipping and looked at the man staring at the camera. There was no question this was Mr. Brewster. He looked sad and old. That picture had to have been taken many years before. The yellowing newspaper was brittle.

"Mr. Brewster. Mr. Brewster, wake up." Manny shook the old man.

Manny had always thought Mr. Brewster was a big, strong man who towered over everyone and everything. Here in his own dining room, his head resting on his chest, Mr. Brewster was frail, vulnerable.

"Yes," Mr. Brewster mumbled, slowly raising his head and staring at Manny. "Is that you, Jimmy?"

"No, it's Emanuel Keefer. Remember?"

Just then the all-clear siren sounded.

"We're having, or we were having, an air-raid drill," he explained quickly. "When you hear the sound, you must turn off all your lights."

Mr. Brewster just stared at Manny. He didn't understand.

"That's okay, Mr. Brewster. I'll just turn off your light now. You can go back to sleep."

Mr. Brewster didn't hear. He was already sleeping. Manny pulled the light cord above the table and left the house, closing the front door quietly behind him. His father was waiting for him in the middle of the street. "Nice job, son. Did you have any problems?"

"No, not really," he said.

"Me either," Dad said. "The Baldwin family had the only house on my side of the street with a light on. They quickly turned it off and were very apologetic."

The morning newspaper was lying at the foot of the porch steps when Manny and his dad got back to their home. His father leaned over and picked it up and as they started up the steps together. "I'm proud of you, son," his dad said while putting his arm around Manny's shoulder. "Thanks for going with me."

Mom, Aunt Etta, and Nora were waiting for them in the kitchen. "How did it go? Such a surprise, and so early in the morning for you two to be out in the cold," his mother said. "You'll both get sick."

"Now, dear, as you know, these are not ordinary times. We're all sacrificing something for each other's safety and the war effort. I think it went just fine. Our street was dark. Manny helped a lot. He had to tell old man Brewster to turn off his light."

His father put the newspaper on the table in front of his chair while he poured a cup of coffee.

"That was no easy trick," Manny said. "He was sound asleep. Mom, did you know he was a baseball pitcher and his son died in World War I?"

"No, I didn't know that. The poor man. No wonder he seems so lonely."

"I knew," Nora said.

Everyone stopped to look at her. "He told me lots of things when we were going through his house looking for metal stuff. He's going to help me win the doll. He's collecting cans. He's got lots of stuff in his basement. I told him Manny would carry it up for me. Right, Manny?"

"Yeah, sure, anything you say, Nora," he answered as he looked over his father's shoulder at the sports page.

"I really like this new sports editor, The Brew. What do you think, Manny?"

"Oh, he's okay."

"Manny knows him," Nora said. "He talks to him all the time."

"How's that?" His father looked at him.

"Oh, um, when I call in the University School scores, he takes them," Manny answered. Manny shot a look at Nora, but she wasn't paying any attention to him.

"Well, listen what he has to say today," his father said. He began to read aloud.

> High school crowds are bigger than ever before. This places an added responsibility on coaches to take all possible precautions not to burn out their young charges in an effort to provide the public with bigger and better teams. Overworking high school players can ruin their ability as athletes later on in life. This should not be overlooked or neglected.

"He seems to care about our youth," Mom said.

"He certainly does. I know our University School wouldn't have gotten its name in the daily paper without him," Dad said.

"Yeah, but he doesn't write anything about the team. Dad, you know Wally Baldwin is a great player, and he doesn't get any publicity."

"You're right. Wally is a natural athlete. I'd like to see him play against this Rachel kid. Have you read about him?"

"A little bit," Manny answered nonchalantly. He looked at Nora. She was busy counting the number of Cheerios in her cereal bowl.

"Well, he plays for this new school out near Hamilton. Last night they played Riley High, wherever that is. Must be another new school. Rachel was in a slump. He had only twenty points."

Manny was amazed that his father knew so much about the

Elmsdale Phantoms. Somehow, it didn't seem right that his own father didn't know that the Elmsdale team didn't exist.

Manny had a funny feeling in his stomach, but he said, "He'd be in a real slump if he played Wally and Felix and the rest of the University School team."

Manny picked up his cereal bowl and walked toward the sink. The editor had printed what he called in. He'd have to wait until later to read the whole article.

"The editor even writes about Syd Rachel in his column today," his father said.

Manny stopped in his tracks. "Oh yeah?" he said. "What does he say?" He hoped he didn't sound too interested.

"The new Elmsdale High School Cagers from near Hamilton boast a crackerjack five led by a smooth guard named Syd Rachel. Rachel averages twenty-three points a game. From what I hear, this tall wonder is too good to be real. He'll be able to show everyone his stuff in the tricounty tournament in two weeks."

His father paused for a second before asking Manny if they could go to the tournament together to see this basketball wonder.

"Sure, Dad, I'd like to. I'd like to see the 'wonder,'" he said, leaving the room to go upstairs to get dressed for work.

Manny walked slowly up the steps. He didn't like the way things were going. Somehow, it was all wrong that his own father believed the stories about the Elmsdale Phantoms. He was beginning to feel just like Wally did—they were picking someone's pocket.

Both Wally and Felix were getting kind of goosey about the whole thing. It was getting harder and harder for him to get them together to plan the next game. Just yesterday, he had stopped by Felix's house to ask a question. Felix wasn't there. His mother explained Wally had dropped by earlier and they had left to meet friends.

"I thought they were meeting you," Felix's mother said.

And then there was Nora. Who knew when she would crack and blow it for all of them?

But we can't stop now, Manny thought. *Somehow, that wouldn't be right either.* He hadn't even had a chance to tell Howard what was going on. Howard would get such a kick out of it. Manny could hear him laughing.

Manny Keefer was not a quitter. And deep down, he knew that if the Elmsdale Phantoms stopped playing now, he might never get to be with Wally and Felix again. The Glutzes needed him more and more at the grocery store. He was afraid he would have to give up the job of team manager. If he did that, he might lose his friends forever. He couldn't let that happen.

CHAPTER 10

WALLY, FELIX, AND THE REST of the team were scrimmaging when Manny arrived at the gym. Ten minutes remained on the clock.

He hated being late, but he couldn't help it. Nora was threatening to tell everybody about the Elmsdale team if he didn't do what she wanted. She insisted that he go over to Mr. Brewster's house with her to look at the scrap metal he had in his basement.

Mr. Brewster had been his typical crabby self. He demanded Manny and Nora wipe their boots on a rug in the mudroom before they came into the house. He made Manny take off his boots before walking into the living room.

Mr. Brewster didn't say anything about the air-raid practice, and Manny didn't mention that he had been in his house. Manny looked into the dining room as they passed by on the way to the cellar. A bowl of artificial fruit sat in the middle of the table. The newspaper clippings that had cluttered the tabletop were nowhere in sight.

Mr. Brewster had stacked at least one hundred cans against the cellar wall. "And I want you to take this," he said as he pointed to an old wrought iron table and chairs. "I was always going to paint that for my wife, but I never did. And here."

He picked up a sled that had the iron runners and a pair of dark, leather skates that had iron blades. "I don't think anyone will use these again. They were my son's and ..." He didn't finish.

Mr. Brewster had gone to a lot of trouble for Nora. "This is great stuff!" Manny exclaimed. "A lot more than we've got at home. I think you'll win that doll, Nora." He gave her a big smile.

"Now don't raise her hopes too high, Emanuel Keefer," Mr. Brewster scolded. "You're always jumping to conclusions, making predictions. We don't know what anybody else has collected. There's a war going on, you know. A lot of people are doing a lot for those boys who are fighting for their country."

Mr. Brewster's outburst shocked Manny. Mr. Brewster was so critical. Manny felt like he had been slapped. Manny wasn't sure why, but he wanted, just once, for Mr. Brewster to approve of something he said or did. But it was obvious that that would never happen, not with this old man.

Nora didn't notice the tension between Manny and Mr. Brewster. Right now, they were her two best friends in the world. "Manny's going to get his friends Wally and Felix to help us carry the stuff to the curb on Saturday," she said.

That was the first time Manny had heard about that. But he said they would. "I've got to go now. The team's practicing, and I'll be late." He started up the cellar steps. "Are you coming, Nora?" he asked.

"No, I'm going to stay with Mr. Brewster. He's teaching me how to play cards. Gin rummy. Maybe we can play together sometime."

"Sure, sometime," Manny said.

Manny sat down in the first row of the bleachers behind the team. He didn't want to bring attention to himself. He was so late. He'd really let the guys down. Coach Ellis would probably fire him as team manager. Manny wouldn't blame him.

He was so deep in thought he didn't notice Rudy Smith sit down next to him. "How ya doin', Manny?" he asked.

"Fine, Rudy. What are you doing here?"

"Taking pictures for the newsletter. We're going to send it to the alumni who are fighting the war," Rudy said.

Rudy was older than Manny and his friends. At six feet, five inches tall, he was very skinny and very clumsy—all arms and legs. He was always running into things or tripping over his own feet. He wasn't an athlete, but he was a photographer and very creative.

"Way to go, Baldwin! Way to go!" Rudy yelled with the cheerleaders after Wally hit the basket from about twenty feet out. "These guys are good," he said to Manny. "The alums fighting overseas will love to read about them. This team needs publicity. Burns me up that the daily newspaper doesn't give us any coverage. Withrow High and Woodward get all the ink. Then there's that new team out near Hamilton with that Dan Pachel or Ratchel, or whatever his name is. He's nothing compared to Wally and Felix. They'd run circles around him."

"His name is Syd, spelled with a *y*, Rachel," Manny said.

"Mmm, what did you say? What do you think of the lighting in here?"

"How do you know about that team?"

"Doesn't everybody? That's all my dad and brother talk about at the breakfast table. My brother saw him play."

"Oh, really? He saw him play?"

"Yep. He said he wasn't as great as the newspaper says."

"Is that so? What's he look like?"

Rudy didn't hear the question over the sound of the buzzer ending the scrimmage. "Hold it a minute, guys! I want to get your picture!" Rudy shouted. As he took one step out onto the floor, his left foot caught the strap of his camera bag that was sitting at his feet.

He tripped and went sliding head first across the shiny, hardwood floor.

"Rudy, are you okay?" Manny jumped up and ran onto the floor. "Are you hurt?"

"Nahh," Rudy said, taking Manny's hand to steady himself as he got up. "Lucky for me I didn't have the school's camera in my hand. I'd be paying for that for a long, long time."

Rudy hurried back to the bleachers to get his camera. "Drat it, the guys are already in the dressing room."

"Can't you catch 'em when they come out?"

"I guess, but I wanted them in their uniforms." He looked around the gym and saw the reserve cheerleaders practicing at the end of the gym. "I'll get some pictures of them first. Ask the guys to wait a minute when they come out, will ya?"

Manny stood on sidelines while Rudy was busy getting group shots with the cheerleaders. On cue, the cheerleaders all smiled.

As he watched, Manny started to formulate a plan. By the time Felix and Wally came out of the dressing room, he knew exactly what they had to do. "Manny, where were you?" Felix asked. "We had a great scrimmage."

"It's a long story. But come here. Quick. I just found our Syd, spelled with a *y*, Rachel."

Manny, Wally, and Felix were huddled, their heads together, whispering, when Rudy walked up to them. "Hey, guys," he said.

"Rudy, my man," Manny said, a big smile on his face. "The guys and I were just talking about you."

"Hey, I'm sorry I didn't get to take a shot of them right after the game."

"They're not upset," Manny said.

"Not a bit, Rudy," Wally added.

"No, Rudy, what we were talking about is the fact that you're such a good—no, a great—photographer," Manny said.

"And we thought, *Hey, he never gets his picture taken,*" Felix added.

Rudy, who hoped they were going to suit up again so he could take their picture, looked taken back by what they were suggesting. Then he said, "That's okay. Photographers don't get their picture taken. They take the pictures."

"Get serious, Rudy," Wally said. "When is the last time you had your picture in the school newspaper?"

"Hmm," he mused. "I don't know that I've ever had my picture in the paper."

"See, that's what we thought," Felix began. "It's time you got some recognition for all your hard work."

Manny said he would take Rudy's picture, which Rudy could then include in the school newsletter that would be sent to the alums fighting for their country.

"That's a good idea, but I don't want to waste the film," Rudy said. "The school owns the camera and buys the film."

"It's not wasting the film," Manny said. "The picture is for the newsletter. It'll have a basketball theme. We'll take a picture of you dribbling the ball or something like that. You can tell us what button to push. We won't hurt the camera."

"Thanks, but no thanks," Rudy said. He started to walk toward the gym door.

"Please, Rudy," Felix called after him.

Rudy shook his head no and kept walking.

"Rudy!" Manny called out. "Felix and Wally will put their uniforms on again if you let us take a picture of you."

That stopped Rudy in his tracks. He turned and walked back to where they were standing.

"Hey, Manny, wait a minute," Wally said. "I'm not changing back into those smelly, wet trunks."

Manny motioned for Wally to be quiet.

When Rudy was within hearing distance, Manny asked, "Well, Rudy, do we have a deal?"

"I don't know. I do need pictures of the guys in action." Rudy paused and stared into space like he was thinking about the answer to Mr. Barton's toughest math question. Finally, he said, "Okay. You can take one picture of me. Let me show you how to work this thing."

"Great," Manny said. He told Wally to run down to the science lab and get Mr. Guenther's tall stool.

"What do you need that for?" Rudy asked.

"You'll see," Manny answered.

"And, here, put this on," Felix said, pulling a wrinkled, smelly team jersey from his gym bag.

"I'm not going to put that on. I'm not on the team. I couldn't dribble the ball if my life depended on it."

"But you are a part of the team," Felix persisted. "You are that all-important sixth man. Without you taking the pictures, no one would know about us. You're getting us recognition."

Rudy liked that idea.

He took off his sweater and put on the jersey while explaining how the camera worked. Manny put his head under the cloth and looked on the camera's ground glass. "Hey, I don't get it. Everything's backward."

"That's what I've tried to explain," Rudy said. "What is on the left, you see as the right. What is on the right, you see on the left. It takes a little time to get used to that."

Manny said a quick prayer that he didn't mess up the shot. This was their only chance to convince The Brew that Syd Rachel did exist.

Rudy didn't hear Wally come back into the gym or see him put the stool about two feet away from the basket hoop and net. "Do you think you've got it?" he asked.

"Show me one more time how to focus it," Manny said.

Manny watched Rudy. "Okay, how far out do I hold the flash?"

"Arm's length," Wally said. "I know that and I'm not even taking the picture."

"Okay, guys. Manny, where do you want me to stand?" Rudy asked. He looked at his watch. "We got to hurry. I promised I'd help my sister pick up stuff for the scrap drive competition."

For a second, Manny forgot about taking the picture. "How much has she collected?" he asked.

"Truck loads. My mom and dad and all my aunts and uncles and grandparents are saving stuff. Mildred wants to win the doll. I know she'll win it. Okay, where do you want me?"

"Over here," Felix called from under the basket. "We want you to stand up on the stool and dunk the ball."

Manny picked up the tripod and moved it closer to the basket. Gently, he put the camera on top of the stand. "I'm going to snap the picture just when you drop the ball in," he said.

"Wait a cotton-pickin' minute," Rudy said, firmly planting his size ten shoes on the basketball court. "I'm not getting up on the stool. I can't.

"Why not?" Wally asked. "We'll help you."

"Nooo, I … I … can't. I'm … Well, I'm very afraid of heights."

"Oh no," Wally mumbled. "I knew this was a dumb idea."

Rudy walked over to where Manny was standing and reached for the camera. "I really have to go."

"Wait a minute, Rudy," Manny said. "I know how it is to be afraid of heights. I am, too. But gosh, as my dad says, we all must sacrifice. These are not ordinary times when we can be ordinary men with ordinary fears. Think of the joy the guys, our alumni who are fighting for our country while they eat food seasoned with red ants, will feel when they see a photographer making a basket."

"You're laying it on a little thick," Wally whispered just loud enough for Manny to hear.

Manny paid no attention. "The caption underneath your photograph could read, 'Ace school photographer dunks ball for winning coverage of the University School fabulous five and the fighting alumni.'"

"Gosh, I don't know," Rudy said. But Manny could tell from the expression on Rudy's face that he was weakening.

Felix saw the look, too. "Come on, Rudy. Here, take my hand."

Rudy brushed aside Felix's hand. He first put one knee on the stool, then the other. He froze in that position.

"Good," Felix said patiently. "Now give me your hand."

Reluctantly, Rudy put out his right arm. Felix grabbed his hand and then yelled to Wally. "Hurry! Get on the other side of him and take his left hand!"

Very carefully, Rudy got to his feet. Once erect, he wobbled like a baby trying to take his first step. "Woooah!" he cried out. "Help me!"

"Grab his legs, Wally," Manny instructed.

Wally wrapped his arms around Rudy's long legs just below the knees, and Rudy seemed frozen. Everyone stood in position while waiting for Rudy to make some gesture that he was okay, that he was still breathing. Finally, he said, "Hey, this isn't so bad," while turning to look at Manny.

The quick movement of his head unsettled him again. "Whooooo," he said.

"Don't look down, Rudy. Look up. Look up at the basket. Good, that's much better. Okay, Felix, give Rudy the basketball."

Felix reached up high so Rudy could keep his eyes on the basket. Wally increased his grip around Rudy's legs. Rudy took the ball from

Felix. But just as Felix let go, so did Rudy. The ball bounced and rolled on the floor toward Manny.

Manny stopped it with his foot and kicked it back toward Felix. Felix picked it up and tried to hand it to Rudy again.

Again, he dropped it.

The ball rolled behind the basket. Manny chased the ball, picked it up, and walked over to his friends.

"Look, Rudy, you're in a hurry, and we're in a hurry. This won't take long. But you've got to hold on to the ball. Just grip the ball with both hands and act like you're going after the greatest dunk shot in the world, the one that wins the game for Elmsdale High. Oh, I mean University School."

"That's easy for you to say, Manny. You should be up here. It's very dangerous."

Manny heard the panic in Rudy's voice. He could see his face was scrunched together like an old potato. Manny walked quickly back to the camera. He put his head under the black cloth, looked through the shutter, focused the lens, and yelled, "Now!"

Rudy dropped the ball on cue, but his aim was bad and the ball hit the rim and ricocheted, almost hitting Wally in the head. Felix ran after the ball. "That's okay, Rudy. We'll try one more."

"But the camera flashed," Rudy yelled.

Felix handed Rudy the ball.

"Rudy, take the ball," Manny said. "Arch your arm like you're going in for your famous hook shot."

"Huh?" Rudy looked at Manny.

"Pretend you're the great basketball star Syd Rachel."

Rudy did exactly as Manny directed. With great flare, he arched his bare, skinny arm. His aim was perfect. Manny's timing was perfect, too. He snapped the picture just as the ball swished through the net.

"That's a take!" Manny shouted.

"Great! It's about time," Wally said. He let go of Rudy's legs.

"Wait! Don't do that!" Rudy yelled. "I'm falling!"

"No, you're not, Rudy," Manny said. "Don't leave him, Wally. Hold on. I'll help."

Rudy was visibly shaken once his shoes hit the hardwood floor. "Rudy, you were great." Manny reached up to put his arm around his shoulder.

But Rudy brushed him off. "That's it. No more," he said. He looked at his watch. "Oh, my gosh, I'm really late. I don't have time to take your pictures," he said apologetically, but it was obvious to everyone he was in no condition to take a picture. All he wanted was to get out of there. "Where's my camera? Where's my bag?"

"No problem. Everything's right here."

While Rudy put his camera away, Manny folded up the tripod. "Got any idea when you'll develop the film?" he asked.

"Soon, very soon," Rudy said, heading for the gym door. "I'll call you."

"Don't forget. I'd like a copy … to show around. I know it's a great shot of you."

As soon as Rudy was out of the gym, Manny turned to Wally and Felix and gave them a big smile. "You guys should've seen his face. He was so scared, he looked mean. Just the way Syd, spelled with a *y*, Rachel would look."

Felix put his arm around Manny's shoulder and told him it was a brilliant idea to take the picture of Rudy and send it to The Brew. When he saw the picture of a real person, he couldn't doubt that Syd with a *y* Rachel or the Elmsdale Phantoms existed.

"Sure," said the ever-doubting Wally. "And what happens if the editor prints the picture and the whole city sees Rudy?"

"Believe me: Rudy doesn't look like Rudy. His mother wouldn't even recognize his picture. He never looks at the sports section. And it's a sure bet his brother won't know him. The name under the picture will be Syd with a *y* Rachel."

The three walked together out of the gym. "You got any ideas what you're going to do about the tournament, oh wise one?" Wally asked. "You sure can't send Rudy."

Manny had to admit the tournament did present a problem. But at least the photograph would buy them time. "Come home with me to discuss it further," Manny suggested. "My mother's cooking tonight, and she always makes plenty. Come on, Wally. You know you love her cooking."

"I can't," Wally said, walking toward the outside door. He stopped and turned. "Are you coming, Felix?"

Felix looked at Wally and then turned to Manny. "Sorry, man. I have to go, too. Maybe tomorrow."

Manny stood alone as his two best friends left the gym. "Yeah, maybe tomorrow."

CHAPTER 11

—⁓—

T HE NEXT FEW DAYS PASSED quickly. When Manny wasn't at Glutz's Grocery Store or at the gym practicing with the guys, he was helping Aunt Etta and Nora. Nora was determined to win the scrap drive contest. Manny did everything he could to encourage her. The more time Nora spent thinking about ways to win, the less time she had to think about the Elmsdale Phantoms. He happily joined in with the rest of the family, thinking of different ways she might gather the scrap she needed to win the contest.

Manny had an idea for a neighborhood soup party. Anyone who contributed to Nora's scrap pile was invited into the house for a bowl of Aunt Etta's delicious World War II soup. At first, Aunt Etta said she couldn't think of making enough soup to feed a neighborhood. But it didn't take much for the family to convince her that her soup could make the difference in Nora getting enough scrap to win the contest. Manny agreed to bring as many of the ingredients as he could from the grocery store. He talked with Mr. Glutz and offered half his week's salary to pay for the cans of beans and tomatoes. But Mr. Glutz wouldn't hear of it. He said the vegetables—and the cans—would be his tickets to bring his family to the Keefer home for Aunt Etta's soup. "You tell me it's the best soup in the world. I must taste it."

Manny's family went without pork, beef, and chicken so they would have enough coupons for the time when Aunt Etta needed the meat and poultry for her soup. Manny designed a flyer that invited neighbors to the Keefer house on Friday evening. He delivered a flyer to every house in a four-block radius. "YOU'RE INVITED" was printed on the outside of each invitation. The inside read, "Just leave your scrap at the curb and come on in to 915 Elm Hill Drive for the gastronomic experience of your life."

Aunt Etta began preparing her specialty on Wednesday. Slabs of pork, beef, and whole chickens simmered in big iron pots on the gas stove for two days. The concoction filled the house with a tantalizing aroma. Everyone in the family dipped into the pot for a spoonful. Nora stood guard over the soup and screeched when she caught someone taking a taste. "Now, honey, we need to taste it to decide if it needs more salt or pepper or spices," Mom explained patiently to Nora when she cried there would be none left for the neighbors.

The afternoon of the party, Manny went straight home after school. He helped Mom set up card tables in each room so the neighbors could sit down. About an hour before the event was to begin, he went outside with the sign. In bold red and black letters, he printed, "Stop here for Aunt Etta's World War II soup."

He was pounding the stake in the ground when he heard a creaking sound behind him. He looked up. Mr. Brewster was pulling a funny-looking, rickety cart across the snow-covered street.

"What's this?" Manny asked. He helped Mr. Brewster pull it up over the curb. "Where did you get it?"

"I made it," Mr. Brewster answered slowly, trying to catch his breath. "I found the buggy wheels in the garage. Can't remember why I had them in the first place. But they came in handy for this."

Manny walked around a contraption that was six feet long and four feet wide. It had wood slats on all four sides. Manny jumped up to try to see what was inside. But he couldn't. Finally, he asked, "What's it for?"

"Nora's scrap drive. What else? The neighbors can put their scrap in the box before they go into your house. Then you—or someone—can pull the cart to school where they'll be weighing everyone's scrap on Saturday."

"That's a great idea, Mr. Brewster. I'd better make another sign. Our neighbors won't know what the cart is for."

"Yes, they will. I plan to stand next to it and tell them."

Manny watched Mr. Brewster slowly make his way back to his house. He hoped Mr. Brewster would put on a sunny disposition before he came back, if he had one. Otherwise, he might scare the neighbors away.

Manny turned to go back into his house. He was almost to the door when he heard someone call his name.

"Keefer, I have something for you."

Manny turned. Rudy was standing on the front sidewalk, straddling his bicycle and waving a manila envelope.

"Rudy, my man. How you doing?" Manny walked nonchalantly out to the sidewalk. He could feel his heart pounding through his thick, wool coat. The moment of truth was near. Was the photograph good enough to fool The Brew?

Rudy handed to him an envelope.

"What's this?"

"You know what it is. It's that ridiculous picture you took of me. I don't know why you took it. No one can tell it's me."

Manny pulled the black-and-white glossy print from the envelope. Rudy was absolutely right. The photograph didn't look a thing like Rudy. Here was a picture of a player from the waist up making the perfect shot—a shot that only Syd with a y Rachel could make.

"Rudy, I don't know what to say."

"You don't have to say anything. The photograph is yours. It is ridiculous. I would never take a picture from that angle. Now you have to live up to your part of the bargain for the team. Set up a special session with the guys in uniform so I can take their picture for the alumni newsletter."

"You have my word. I'll do it as soon as I can."

Rudy started to leave. "World War II soup? What's that?"

"It's a Keefer secret." Manny smiled. "Bring over any scrap you have around the house, drop it in the cart, and come on in and find out for yourself."

Rudy explained there wasn't an ounce of scrap metal around his house since his sister also was competing in the scrap drive at school. "Nobody will beat Mildred," he said, riding away. "Better tell your sister that she doesn't have a chance."

"Don't be so sure of that!" Manny called after him, waving the manila envelope. "And you're missing the best bowl of soup ever."

Manny didn't like to hear about Mildred's collection drive. Maybe he'd better warn Nora she had stiff competition. He didn't want her to be too disappointed.

Before he had a chance, the neighbors started ringing the doorbell. For the next two hours, Manny was stuck at the kitchen sink, washing and drying the dishes for the next batch of neighbors. At one point, when he was caught up on his work, he put on his coat and cap and went out to the front yard to check on Mr. Brewster. The old man still stood in the dark night. From a distance, he looked like a stone statue. Manny didn't mean to sneak up on him, but the man jumped when Manny asked, "How are we doing? We're almost out of soup. We must have a cart full of scrap."

"Afraid not, Emanuel. A lot of people have dropped in only a few cans. They apologized but said a girl named Mildred asked for their scrap weeks ago. They cleaned out their attics and cellars for her."

"Mildred. She's a real pain. I know her brother. He can be a pain, too. He told me she's been working for weeks. He's already taken several loads to school. But he didn't tell me that she was working our neighborhood. That's not fair."

"Now, Emanuel, there's nothing fair or unfair about it. You're forgetting the whole point of why the United States is collecting scrap," Mr. Brewster began his lecture. "Not only does the government need the metal for machinery, it's a great way for all of us back home to rally behind the boys who are risking their lives for us. It helps not to feel so helpless."

"I know. I know." Manny was impatient. He hated it when Mr. Brewster lectured. "That's not why I came out here. I'll relieve you so you can go inside, warm up, and have a bowl of Aunt Etta's soup before it's all gone. Believe me: it is very, very tasty."

"I know. Nora brought me a bowl about an hour ago. I'm ready to go home. No one has come by in the past fifteen minutes. I'll push the cart to my garage for safe keeping tonight."

Manny offered to push the cart for him, but Mr. Brewster refused. "Okay, if you're sure," Manny said. "Do you know what time it is?"

Mr. Brewster pushed back the sleeve of his heavy coat with his gloved hand. He walked a few feet to his right where the gas streetlight cast its glow. "I have exactly 6:57."

His voice was strong, but Manny noticed that his hand was shaking. Mr. Brewster looked as vulnerable and frail tonight as he had the night of air-raid drill. Manny wanted to order him into the house where he would be warm. But he knew Mr. Brewster wouldn't listen to him.

Manny hurried back into the house. During the party, he had made a quick telephone call to The Brew. He wanted to tell him that the Elmsdale Phantoms wouldn't be playing tonight. But the reporter who answered the telephone said The Brew was out of the office, covering the Withrow-Woodward game, and wasn't expected back in the office until after ten o'clock.

That's when Manny decided tonight would be the perfect time to deliver the photograph to the newspaper office. He could put the envelope on The Brew's desk, no questions asked.

Manny hung his coat and cap on the wall hook and started up the steps. "Is that you, Manny?" his father called from the dining room.

"Yes," Manny said. He backed down the steps and walked into the dining room.

Dad, Mom, Aunt Etta, and Nora were sitting at the table with the Warrens and Barons. "Sam Baron tells me that he saw this Rachel kid play with that new team outside Hamilton," Dad began.

"Really?" Manny said, sitting down at the table.

"Yes. He says that the kid is terrific. Did you tell me you saw him play?"

"Ah yes. I mean no. I mean I've heard about him, but I've never actually seen him play."

"Someone told me that he wasn't as good as everybody says," his father continued.

"I might have told you one of Mr. Glutz's customers saw him," Manny offered.

"It doesn't matter who told me. I told Sam that you and I are going to the all-city tournament to watch him. Sam wants to go with us. Can you buy the tickets through University School?"

"I guess I can. You know University School wasn't invited to the tournament."

"I wouldn't expect that, Manny," his father said. "The University School team is a fine team—"

"That's right," Sam Baron chimed in. "The University School gives its fans—the parents and the students—a lot of enjoyment. But no one expects the team to compete in a league with these big public schools."

"I think Wally and Felix and the rest of the guys would beat Withrow or Woodward," Manny said.

77

"No one said they couldn't," Dad said. He was surprised that Manny was so argumentative.

Aunt Etta interrupted the conversation when she asked if anyone wanted more soup. Mr. Baron said he would, holding up his bowl. Manny's father took more as well, saying he didn't want to see it go to waste.

Manny took the opportunity to leave the room and hurry upstairs. He stood by his door a long minute to make sure Nora had not followed him before he closed it behind him. Because it didn't have a lock, he propped the back of his desk chair under the doorknob. He didn't want anyone walking into the room.

He fell to his knees and with his right arm reached under the bed until his hand touched the box. Quickly, he pulled it out and placed it on top of the bed.

The room was dark. He turned on the lamp that stood on his night table just long enough to find, in the table drawer, the flashlight his dad had given him for air-raid drills.

Manny hopped on the bed and rested the box on his lap. Then he piled his pillows one on top of the other and rested the flashlight at the top of the mound so its light shone directly on top of the box. This was the box where he kept Howard's letters and his wallet that he had asked Manny to keep until his return.

Manny pulled the envelope holding the photograph out from under the blanket where he had hurriedly placed it after Rudy gave it to him. He had almost gotten caught with it when he was rushing up the steps before the crowd of neighbors arrived for the scrap drive. "Where are you going so fast, young man?" Mrs. Cann, Felix's mother, called up to him.

Manny stopped and balanced himself on one step as he turned. "Oh, hi, Mrs. Cann. Nowhere really, but I have to hurry. Is Felix coming for soup?"

"No, not tonight. He and Wally went with some of the team to the citywide basketball game tonight."

"That's right. I forgot," Manny said, continuing to run up the steps. But he hadn't forgotten. They had not invited him to go with them. *I wouldn't have been able to go with them anyway with the scrap drive going on,* he tried to reason with himself.

He felt inside the box for a pencil and notepad. Then he pulled the photograph out of the envelope and held it under the light. "Perfect," he whispered to himself.

He placed the lid back on the box to use as a flat surface to write his note.

"To The Brew," he started. "No, that's not good," he said. He crumbled the piece of notepaper into a ball, aimed it for the waste can in the corner of the room, and flipped it just right. "That's good for two," he said when he heard the paper hit the bottom of the can.

"Dear Sir," he started again. "This is a photograph of the great Syd Rachel. (Don't forget to spell Syd with a *y.)* The photographer snapped this as Rachel went in for his famous dunk shot. He is the best of all the rest. Thanking you in advance for publishing his picture."

Manny paused. How could he sign it? He couldn't use his real name. The Brew didn't even know his name, and he never asked for a name when he called in the game scores. Manny looked at his watch. He had to hurry. The Brew would be back in the office soon.

"Manny, are you upstairs?" his mother called from the foot of the steps. "We need you down here."

Manny jumped off the bed and pulled the chair away from the door. "Yes, Mom, I'm here," he answered as nonchalantly as he could.

"Dear, everyone is gone. We need your help cleaning up."

"But Mom," he protested. He had to take the photograph to the newspaper office tonight.

"No buts, Emanuel. I need you downstairs now."

79

"I'm coming." He switched on the night table light, reread the letter, and then printed, "Sincerely, Your friend and a big Elmsdale fan." He slipped the note into the envelope with the photograph, sealed the envelope, and put it back under his blanket. Then he shoved the box under the bed and went downstairs.

He would have to deliver the photograph to the newspaper office before he went to work the next morning.

CHAPTER 12

MANNY WAS OUT OF THE house by 7:15 the next morning so he could catch the same trolley Dad, Mom, and Aunt Etta rode downtown on weekdays. The trolley stopped three blocks from *The Daily News* office building. Manny had to hurry. He had exactly twenty minutes to deliver the photograph and get back to the trolley stop.

The newspaper building was the tallest building on the block. *"The Daily News"* was engraved in stone above the revolving door. Manny pushed the door with all his strength until it opened into a large marble lobby. Elevators lined both sides of the wall. This was not what Manny expected. He looked around for a clue for where he should go.

"You look lost. Can I help you?" a voice asked.

Manny jumped at the sound. He turned in a full circle before he saw the uniformed guard sitting behind a desk. "Yes, um," Manny stuttered. "I'm looking for the sports department. I'm looking for The Brew."

"Sports is on the tenth floor."

Manny thanked him and started toward the elevator.

"Hold on, son. There's no one in the office now, and I can't let you go up in the elevator."

"But I have something for The Brew. It's very important that he gets it."

"I'm sure it is important. But The Brew will not be here until this afternoon. He covers basketball games at night. He doesn't come in until after four and leaves after midnight."

"But I must give him this photograph." Manny was beginning to panic. He sounded like Nora did all the time. He couldn't believe his bad luck. First, Mom wouldn't let him leave the house last night. Now, the sports department was closed. If he didn't get the photograph to The Brew now, he never would. This might be the end of the line for the Elmsdale Phantoms. Syd, spelled with a *y*, Rachel was beginning to fade into the distance.

"I'll see that The Brew gets it, son," the guard said. "Put his name on the envelope. Will he know who it's from?"

"Yes, sir. I have a note inside," Manny said. He borrowed the guard's pencil to print, "The Brew," in bold letters. He handed the envelope to the man then started to walk toward the door. He turned. "You won't forget, will you?"

"I won't forget. You have my word."

Manny had to run all the way to the trolley stop, but he made it in time.

A line the width of the store was waiting for Mr. Glutz to open up when Manny arrived with two minutes to spare.

The morning passed quickly. Manny was busy stocking shelves, delivering orders, and helping Mr. Glutz behind the meat counter. He had little time to think about the Elmsdale Phantoms or his adventure to the newspaper office.

"Are you going to take time out for a sandwich today?" Mr. Glutz asked during a lull about two o'clock. They had been so busy that Manny hadn't even thought about food, but now that Mr. Glutz mentioned it, he was hungry. Mr. Glutz fixed their usual baloney sandwiches while Manny got two bottles of root beer from the icebox.

They both sat settled down on tall stools behind the counter.

"Really something about this fake basketball team," Mr. Glutz said between bites.

"What team is that?" Manny asked, picking up a slice of bread to see if Mr. Glutz had remembered to put mustard on his sandwich.

"That school out near Hamilton. You know, the winningest team in the tristate with the superstar Ratcell or whatever his name is."

Manny dropped his sandwich on the floor. "Syd with a *y* Rachel," he mumbled as he got down off the stool and picked up the sandwich. Little pieces of sawdust from the wooden floor now dotted his bread.

"Don't eat that," Mr. Glutz said. "I'll fix you another sandwich."

"No, it's okay, Mr. Glutz." He took another bite from his sandwich. "Mmmm, good," he said, but he almost gagged. Quickly, he took a swig of root beer.

Mr. Glutz chuckled. He took another bite of sandwich and a sip of root beer, too. "Yep, guess somebody made up the whole thing. They'll be in a lot of trouble when they get caught."

As soon as Manny was sure his voice wouldn't quiver, he said, "I'm not sure I know what you're talking about, Mr. Glutz."

"Here," Mr. Glutz said. He reached for the afternoon newspaper that was lying on the counter. It was already folded to the sports section. "Read it for yourself. The headline says, 'Ghosts Now Perform on Basketball Court. Heralded Elmsdale a Little Team That's Not There.'"

Manny's hand was shaking when he took the paper from Mr. Glutz. He started to read it to himself. "Read it aloud, if you would, Manny."

He started reading. "Columbus, Ohio. Bit of basketball mystery-drama entitled 'The Ghost Team of Butler County or the Little School That Wasn't There!'"

"What's Columbus got to do with this?" Mr. Glutz asked.

"It means that the reporter, Tom Moore, is working out of the state capital for the Associated Press, a national news wire service."

Manny looked up. A man whom he had never seen before was standing at the counter with his own newspaper. "It means this story was printed in newspapers all over the state, maybe even the country."

"You mean people are reading this story everywhere?" Manny was shocked and scared.

"Go on, Manny. Keep reading," Mr. Glutz said.

Manny said,

> Early this week, a Cincinnati newspaper featured the following item: "Little Elmsdale High School, located on Route 4 near Hamilton, is claiming outstanding success in the first year the farm lads have tried basketball. Elmsdale has won nine straight, the latest a 42–25 thrashing of Riley. Syd Rachel is Elmsdale's star and quite a cage man he is. In six games, Rachel has chalked up 140 points. His effort against Riley was a mere high-point job of 23 points. Ted Muehlenkamp, another good shot for Elmsdale, who would possibly star on any other team, is somewhat dwarfed by Rachel."
>
> Now we've been shuffling scholastic cage and grid teams for several years, and that Elmsdale school didn't strike a responsive chord in our memory. We had a hunch it wasn't one of Ohio's Class B or Class C institutions. So we donned our rubber-soled shoes, grabbed our magnifying glass, and started sleuthing. Telephone calls about Elmsdale brought these answers: H. R. Townsend, state high school athletic commissioner: "Never heard of an Elmsdale High School."

State Department of Education: "There's no such school in Ohio."

Supt. C. H. Williams, Butler County Schools: "There's no Elmsdale School in this county. Nearest thing we have is Williamsdale, but it doesn't have a high school. If you find an Elmsdale, please let me know about it, for I'd like to know where it is, too."

Then we checked up on Riley, the latest victim of the elusive Elmsdale. It seems there is a Relly High School in Butler County, but that team lost to unbeaten Hanover last week and has never heard of Elmsdale, Rachel, or Muehlenkamp.

The only Riley in the state is Riley Township of Pandora, up in Putnam County, 135 miles from Hamilton. Class B teams in their first year of competition just don't travel that far.

Not only that, but the US postal guide shows, in all the forty-eight states, there is not one Elmsdale post office. Right there we started to suspect, Sherlock Holmes that we are, that someone had tried to slip one over on the press."

Once he started reading, Manny never looked up. When he finished, he dropped the paper to his side and stood quietly behind the meat counter.

"Somebody played a joke on the whole city," the stranger at the counter said.

Manny looked. The counter was lined with customers who had been listening to him read the article.

"Funny though," someone else said.

"And it was fun to read about a new little school that had a bunch of farm kids who were outstanding athletes. I planned to get down to the city tournament just to see their big star play. What's his name?"

"Syd with a *y* Rachel," Manny said softly.

Mr. Glutz told everyone that he had hoped they would play the University School because they would have beaten them.

"It wouldn't have happened," Manny whispered.

"You're right about that, son. The Elmsdale team never existed."

Mr. Glutz laughed. Some of the others at the counter laughed, too.

Manny walked slowly back to the middle of the store where he started stocking shelves. He was deep in thought when he felt a tap on his shoulder. He turned.

"Did you see it?" Felix whispered, looking to see if anybody was in the aisle with them.

"Did you see the article?" Wally asked in a loud, accusing voice before Manny could answer.

"Shhh," Felix admonished Wally.

"Yes, I read it," Manny said quietly.

"Do you think they know who did it?" Wally asked again too loudly.

"Shhhh," Manny cautioned. "We can't talk here. Come over to my house at eight tonight."

But Wally was insistent. "What do you think will happen to us?"

"Nothing's going to happen to us, if you don't blow it now by talking too much," Manny said. "We didn't do anything criminal. We were just having fun."

Manny thought of the conversation he had just heard between Mr. Glutz and some of his customers. They admitted that they enjoyed reading about the team. And whoever was responsible, well, it was harmless fun.

Manny's voice was strong, but there was an edge to it. He was trying to convince himself. "Come on over to my house tonight and we'll talk about it."

"We can't," Wally grumbled.

"That's right, Manny," Felix said. "We have an out-of-town game tonight. We won't be back until late."

Manny had forgotten. He told the coach he wouldn't be able to travel with the team because he was working. Coach Ellis didn't like it, but he didn't say anything.

"Oh, that's right. How about tomorrow?" Manny asked.

"We'll see," Wally said.

"I'll call you," Felix said.

Manny stood and once again watched his two best friends in the world walk away without saying good-bye. "Good luck tonight!" he called after them.

Just as they reached the door to go out, Rudy was walking in. "Hey, guys," Rudy greeted them. "Have you decided on a time when I can get your photo? Manny said he would set it up. Maybe tomorrow?"

"I don't know when," Felix said.

"Ask big shot, know-it-all Keefer," Wally stormed. "He's over there."

Manny and Rudy stood at the window and watched Wally and Felix walk down the street. "Golly, what did I do?" Rudy asked. "I feel like I've walked into a hornet's nest."

"It's not you, Rudy. It's me."

"Does this mean I won't get my picture?"

"Don't worry. You'll get the photo." Manny assured him.

"Will you be there?" Rudy asked.

"No. I'm resigning as manager."

CHAPTER 13

MANNY HELPED MR. GLUTZ WASH the inside of the meat counter before he left for the weekend. He was in no hurry to go home.

He trudged through the snow with a heavy heart. He tried to walk slowly, but it was too cold. He pushed his bare hands deep into his coat pockets.

Manny considered walking around the block to avoid going through Mr. Brewster's yard, but his face and hands were numb. And it didn't matter, not at this time of night. The old man would never see him in the dark. He climbed over the fence around Mr. Brewster's yard. A light shining in Mr. Brewster's kitchen cast a glow on the snow. Manny walked to the side of the yard so Mr. Brewster couldn't see him if he just happened to look out the window. Manny was almost to the front sidewalk when someone turned on the porch light and opened the front door.

"Who's out there? I say, 'Who's out there?'"

Manny stood still as a snowman. Maybe, if he didn't move, Mr. Brewster would give up and go back inside his house.

But this wasn't Manny's day in more ways than one. Mr. Brewster walked to the side of the porch and shined his flashlight right in Manny's face. "Is that you, Emanuel Keefer? I should have known."

"Yes, Mr. Brewster," Manny said. "It was just so cold that—"

"Don't give me any excuses. Even if it's cold, you could have answered me. Now come here. I want to talk with you."

Manny couldn't believe it. As if he didn't feel bad enough already, now he had to listen to Mr. Brewster lecture him about what an awful person he was. And tonight Manny would have to agree with him. The only good thing about it was that talking with Mr. Brewster would prolong his going home.

Manny walked slowly onto the porch. Mr. Brewster waited by the door. "Come inside. It's too cold to stand out here. I need to talk with you."

"Mr. Brewster, about cutting through your yard—" Manny began.

"Emanuel Keefer, hush about the yard. I just don't like seeing movement in my backyard and not knowing who it is. But that's not why I called you in. In fact, I'm happy to see you."

"Happy?" Manny said as he followed Mr. Brewster into the dining room. He didn't think he'd ever make Mr. Brewster happy. Something told him that happy wasn't exactly what he meant.

The small chandelier above the dining room table cast an eerie light in the large room with the high ceiling. Newspaper clippings covered the table just as they had the first time Manny was in this room. Newspapers were scattered on the floor near Mr. Brewster's chair.

The old man eased his stiff body into the captain's chair at the head of the table and motioned for Manny to sit down in the chair next to him.

As Manny waited for Mr. Brewster to say something, he noticed that that afternoon newspaper was lying on the table in front of Mr. Brewster. It was turned to the sports page.

Oh no, he thought. *Surely, Mr. Brewster doesn't know about Elmsdale and Syd with a y Rachel. Or does he?*

"Manny, as you probably know, Nora didn't win the scrap drive. That little girl by the name of Mildred won. Nora was a distant second."

"Gosh, no, I didn't," Manny said, overcome with relief that Mr. Brewster didn't want to talk about Elmsdale.

"She is very upset," Mr. Brewster said.

"Gosh, I bet she is. I haven't seen her. I've been working. But I feel terrible, too." That certainly was the truth. Tonight Manny knew all about the pain of losing.

Mr. Brewster looked closely at Manny. "We all feel for her. She had her heart set on winning. I thought she had a pretty good chance. Now, mind you, there's nothing wrong with coming in second. That's very good. And the reason for collecting the scrap is important. It gives everyone a chance to do something and not just sit back doing nothing in this war."

"You're right, Mr. Brewster."

"I feel like I let Nora down," Mr. Brewster said. "I should have gone door to door with her at least in this neighborhood. That's where Mildred got a lot of her scrap."

"You can't blame yourself." Manny suddenly felt sorry for Mr. Brewster and Nora as well as himself.

Mr. Brewster sat with his chin on his chest for a long minute. When he looked up again, Manny thought he might be crying.

"So that's why I made this decision," Mr. Brewster said. He leaned down, picked up a very large box that was at the side of his chair, and put the box in front of Manny. "Go ahead. Open it, Emanuel."

Manny stood up, opened the flaps on the top of the box, and peered inside. There, lying wrapped in tissue paper, was one of the biggest dolls he had ever seen in his life.

"It's the same doll they gave the winner of the scrap drive," Mr. Brewster said. "I went downtown and talked with old man Benson, who owns the five-and-dime store. He stocked two of the dolls. Do you think Nora will like it?"

"Oh, Mr. Brewster, she'll love it."

"I want you to take it to her tonight."

Manny looked at Mr. Brewster. "Hey, wait a minute. Did I hear you correctly? You went downtown?"

"Haven't been there in I don't know how long." Mr. Brewster leaned back in his chair, smiling to himself. "Lot of things have changed. Some haven't."

"I can't take the doll to Nora, Mr. Brewster," Manny said. "You should do it. Come on. Let's go now."

"I can't do that."

"Why not? You went downtown."

"Not tonight. Maybe tomorrow."

"Well, you'll have to do it, Mr. Brewster," Manny said. He folded his arms sternly. "You have to do it, because I won't." With that, he got up from his chair and started to put on his coat. "I've got to go. It's late. I haven't eaten." He started toward the door.

"Sit down, Emanuel. There's something else we need to talk about."

Manny turned to look at Mr. Brewster. He was holding the afternoon paper in his hands. Manny walked slowly back to the table and sat down again in the same chair.

"I suspect you've read this," Mr. Brewster said, pointing to the article.

"Yes, sir," he said, realizing his worst nightmare was coming true.

"I've been following this Elmsdale team with its star Syd Rachel for some time now," the old man began. "I first got interested when little Miss Nora started talking about a team that her brother Manny and his friends had created. At first, I didn't understand what she was talking about. I thought it was some imaginary game she was playing. She misses her brother Howard and I thought it had something to do with him. Nora was never sure what was going on, but she knew she was a part of Manny's gang, doing something that was fun. She said she couldn't tell me because she had promised. She said she might choke if she said too much."

Manny sat and listened. His chin rested on his chest.

Mr. Brewster continued. "I was quite taken by this Elmsdale team myself. As was my son."

"Your son?" Manny looked at the clippings on the table. He remembered reading that night about a soldier who had died in World War I. "I thought your son was dead."

"That was my older son, John. I think you might know my younger son, Jimmy."

"Know him? How would I know him?"

With that, Manny was suddenly aware that there was someone else in the room—someone walking in from the kitchen.

"You're right, Manny. We really don't know each other, do we? We've never met. But, I'd recognize your voice anywhere."

Manny looked up. There stood a tall, young man, maybe in his early thirties, with a sad look on his face. Manny took a long hard look. He recognized the man from the photo that ran next to his sports column in the newspaper. "You're The Brew," he said quietly.

Manny suddenly was sick inside. The whole world would know what he had done. He could see the headlines in the paper. "Emanuel Keefer, the kid who tried to put something over on the city."

"Yes, he's The Brew, but I know him better as my son Jimmy," Mr. Brewster said. The Brew sat down at the table next to Manny. Mr. Brewster continued talking as if Manny wasn't there. He never took his eyes off his son.

"Dad, let me—"

"No, son, I want to start."

"Jimmy, The Brew, came to this house today, not long after the afternoon paper hit the streets. He hasn't been here since his mother died. I haven't talked with him in five years. He knocked so gently on the door that I didn't hear him at first. Then, when I did, I didn't want to open it. But then I thought it might be Nora, so I called out, 'Who is it? Who's there?' A second later, the answer came. 'It's Jimmy, Dad. May I come in?'"

Mr. Brewster was silent. Manny waited.

"At first I didn't want him to come in, but then I opened the door. He wiped his feet on the mat without me telling him to and followed me into the dining room. He sat where you are sitting and handed me this paper. He told me what had happened. He told me he had been taken in by a practical joke. He said he would be the laughingstock of the city. He said he might even lose his job."

Manny jumped up. "Oh no, I wouldn't let that happen," he said, looking directly at The Brew. "I'll talk to your boss. I'll tell them it is all my fault."

The Brew smiled at Manny and motioned for him to sit down again. "That won't be necessary, Manny. I've already talked with him. I'm not getting fired. But I am going to write a column and try to explain to my readers what happened. And when you think about it, what harm was done?"

"The harm is that the team was really a lie. Like Wally said, what we did was pick someone's pocket. We were all wrong, but mostly I was wrong. I had the most fun. I thought I was so smart."

Neither the Brewsters nor Manny spoke. Again, the room was quiet.

Finally, Mr. Brewster said, "Why did you do it, Emanuel?"

Manny thought for a moment, then began. "In the beginning, I was mad at The Brew," he said while looking directly at the sports editor. "I thought, no offense, you were a fool. If you couldn't recognize the University School team, then I'd show you. And—"

"Wait. Hold on a minute," The Brew interrupted. "What do you mean I didn't recognize the University School team?"

Manny explained that when he first called him at the beginning of the season, The Brew had told him that the small private school team wouldn't rate more than a line or two on the results of their games.

The Brew looked shocked. "I never thought of it that way, that the small private school teams would think I didn't believe they rated more than a line or two. I certainly don't feel that way," The Brew said. "I'm the only one in the sports department with all the other men and women off fighting for the country. I thought I had to concentrate on the bigger, better schools since there was only me. I had only so much time."

"But the University School team is really, really, really good! They could have beaten the Phantoms any day!" Manny exclaimed.

The Brewsters started to laugh. Manny joined them when he realized what he had said. "I mean, they would have beaten them if they were real."

Manny was beginning to feel better about the situation until he remembered Wally and Felix, his two best friends in the world. "I was really mad at you in the beginning," he said, "but I continued the joke because I wanted to be a part of the team. I wanted to be Wally and Felix's friend forever. I was afraid if we didn't have basketball in common we wouldn't have any reason to be friends."

Mr. Brewster waited before he replied. Then he measured his words. "With certain people, we always have a reason to be friends, Emanuel." He pushed his chair back from the table, got up slowly, and walked over to Manny. He put his hand on his shoulder. "It's getting late, son. You'd best go home now."

The Brew got up from his chair, too. "What's going to happen now?" Manny asked.

"Well, now, that's an interesting question," The Brew said. "Guess you'll have to wait and read what it says in tomorrow's paper."

Manny walked down the steps. He was halfway down the walk

when he remembered. He turned and saw Mr. Brewster still standing at the door. "I forgot the doll. I'll take it to Nora."

"That won't be necessary. I'll bring the doll to her myself. You are right. I should do it. It'll be early in the morning. Jimmy is going to pick me up and take me to his house for dinner with his family."

"It will be the first time he sees his grandson. He's named after his uncle John."

"Good night, Eman—" Mr. Brewster stopped. "Good night, Manny."

CHAPTER 14

MANNY TOOK HIS TIME WALKING across the street to his house. His head was filled with all kinds of thoughts. He didn't know why The Brew hadn't visited his father for years. But for whatever reason, they seemed to have resolved their differences.

He was happy to know that The Brew wouldn't be losing his job. He would have to wait until the morning newspaper to know where he stood in the situation. Would The Brew reveal his name as the mastermind for the deception? If he did reveal it, what would Manny say to his family? How could he defend himself? He was almost resigned to the fact that he would never be friends with Wally and Felix again. But would his very own parents desert him too?

Manny switched on the overhead light when he walked into the kitchen. He made his way through the dark dining room to the hallway and started up the steps. He stopped halfway up when he heard Aunt Etta reading out loud to Nora. He crept down the steps and walked back to the kitchen. Mom had left a note leaning against an empty glass that was sitting on the table next to a plate and silverware.

> We're at the Josephs' playing pinochle. Heat up your dinner.
> Love and kisses,

Mom.

PS Letter from Howard on the mantel.

"A letter from Howard," he said to himself, running back into the living room. He found the familiar white envelope leaning against the mirror behind the mantel. Mom and Dad had given Howard the stationery at the train depot the day he left home more than a year ago.

Manny poured himself a glass of milk before he started to read the one-page letter.

Howard didn't have much to say. He was sorry he hadn't written sooner, but the military kept everyone very busy.

> The most exciting thing here is the fact I have to strain my tea with my teeth. Ho. Ho. Disgusting. What's happening back home? I want to hear about everything. Don't spare the details.
> Love,
> Howard

Manny read the letter three times, clinging to every word, before he heated up his supper. He picked up the letter again when had finished eating and read it through a fourth time.

He made his decision. "I gotta do it. Right, Duncan?" he asked the dog, who had been at his side since he came in the back door.

Manny had waited weeks for Howard's new address. Carefully, he had cut every article about the Elmsdale High School Phantoms from the morning newspaper and stashed them carefully in the box under his bed. He had rehearsed in his mind all the funny things he would tell Howard about the great Phantom basketball team.

Now he had the address, but the game was over. He could forget the whole thing. But not to tell Howard would be like telling a lie. He had to tell Howard. He needed advice about how he could win back Wally and Felix's friendship.

He found a notebook and pencil in the buffet drawer. He sat down at the head of the oak dining room table, as he did when he and Felix and Wally and Nora were a team creating a team.

He looked around the room. Everything was the same, but not the same. Then he felt Duncan rest his head on his foot under the table. He had never done that before, but somehow, it was comforting and gave Manny the courage to start writing.

Dear Howard. How are you? We were worried about you.

Howard, there is something I must tell you. It all started when I saw this newspaper article …

Manny didn't know how long he sat at the table. The next thing he remembered was waking up in his bed to the muffled sounds of his family downstairs in the dining room. Rays of morning sun danced on the bedroom ceiling. The enticing smell of bacon frying in the skillet filled the room.

And then he remembered. Today he would have to tell everyone about the phantom basketball team. He would have to confess.

Manny wanted to stay in bed. But the bacon smelled too good and he was very hungry. He went downstairs. "Good morning, everyone," he said. "Gosh, it's late. Why didn't someone wake me?" He poured himself a glass of milk.

"Good morning, son," his father said from behind the newspaper.

"Look, Manny. Look at my doll."

The doll in its frilly, pink, organdy dress filled the chair next to Nora.

"Wow, that's a neat doll, Nora. Where did you get it?"

"Mr. Brewster brought it over to me this morning. He said I worked so hard that I deserved a doll too. Isn't it wonderful? There are only two dolls in the whole city like her. Mildred Smith has the other one. I called her up and she is coming over this afternoon to play."

"I thought you didn't like Mildred," Manny said to Nora. But he never took his eyes off his father. He wondered what Jimmy Brewster had written about the Elmsdale team and the article in the Saturday afternoon paper.

"Oh, she's okay. I'd like to be her friend. Our dolls can be friends too. They can be twins like Ted and Tim."

"What twins do you know?" Mom asked Nora. She put a plate heaped with six pieces of bacon, scrambled eggs, and toast in front of Manny.

He was just about to pop the first forkful in his mouth when his father said, "Nice article about University School's win last night."

"Really? We got … I mean, the guys got some press?"

His father didn't hear the question. Instead, he said, "Listen to The Brew's column. He's responding to the article in the afternoon paper about the phantom basketball team. Did you read that article, Manny?"

"Hasn't everybody?"

"Listen to what The Brew has to say in his column this morning. 'I read our competition's story about the ghosts that now perform on our basketball courts with great interest.'"

Manny put his fork down and sat up in his chair. Duncan rested his head on Manny's right foot. But it didn't make Manny feel any better.

Dad continued quoting the newspaper:

As you all know, this paper and this editor have given a lot of coverage to the new Elmsdale High Phantoms. We were all taken in by their star Syd Rachel, the Muehlenkamp twins, and Willie Feldhouse. From the beginning, the team seemed bigger than life itself. I wanted their winning streak to go on forever.

But at the same time, I was wishing deep down that one of our city teams would beat them. Maybe their first defeat would come in overtime during the all-city basketball tournament, I mused.

Now we find out that the Elmsdale Phantoms and Syd Rachel and the Muehlenkamp twins never existed. I don't doubt that. But I questioned why someone felt compelled to create this team and call this newspaper. I can remember the young voice that called me religiously after each game. I remember that voice full of fun and pride at what the Elmsdale High Phantoms were achieving on the basketball court. I believe it was that enthusiastic voice that made me a believer.

Dear readers, I heard that young voice again. This time the voice was filled with remorse, sadness, and defeat. But still, that voice, who I now know belongs to Emmanuel 'Manny' Keefer, a spunky, young sophomore at University School, had the courage to tell me face-to-face exactly why he did what he did. The young Keefer called me on the telephone to tell me about his amazing school team with its talented players. But I blew him off. He says I said I would run the score of the team's games but not a box score or article because the school wasn't big enough for full coverage. If I left him with that impression, I apologize.

With most of our talented newspaper staff helping fight this war, I am a one-man show with little time to cover every team as it should be covered. But young Keefer got me thinking. I went to my editor with my idea, which he approved. Beginning next Saturday, we will have a full page of high school sports. And I'm asking young Keefer to join me as an assistant to help take the information over the phone and write some of the stories. I hope other schools will have stringers for their teams call in the scores and other information on their games.

In the meantime, I have a sneaking suspicion that Manny Keefer and I will make a good team. We hope you think so too.

Manny's father stopped reading. He looked at Manny. "I don't know what to say, son," he began.

"I was wrong, Dad. I know. I just hope you and Mom and Aunt Etta and everybody can forgive me. I will do the best I can working with The Brew."

Silence filled the room. Then Nora, who no one thought was listening while playing with her doll, said, "Well, as we are always saying, these aren't ordinary times."

Everyone laughed. Together they repeated, "These aren't ordinary times."

Manny let his eyes fall on the long, shiny, hardwood table that was spotlighted by the morning sun. For a brief moment, he saw Syd, spelled with a *y*, Rachel, the Muehlenkamp twins, George Wynn, and Willie Feldhouse in their full-court press. They were smiling. For one magical moment, the fabulous Phantom Five were back.

AUTHOR'S NOTE

The piece of basketball mystery-drama entitled "The Ghost Team" or the "Little School That Wasn't There" is a true story. The names, of course, were changed to protect the not-so-innocent, who enjoyed a friendship that thrived for half a century and spanned from one end of the country to the other.

DISCUSSION QUESTIONS

1. Could students today create a basketball team, telephone the information to a newspaper reporter, and then see the false information printed in the next day's newspaper? Discuss.

2. Did Manny intend to lie about the fake team? Was he wrong? Was it worth it?

3. What caused him to be truthful in the end? Is that a good reason?

4. In the story, Nora asks what "Loose lips sink ships" means. But no one answers her. What do you think it means? Why was this a fear in our country? Discuss.

5. What was Nora saving, and why? Is it important to recycle today? Why? What does your family recycle?

6. Is it necessary to make sacrifices for your country today? If yes, what sacrifices in your everyday life are you willing to make?

CPSIA information can be obtained at www.ICGtesting.com
Printed in the USA
BVOW02s0543010515

398436BV00001B/3/P